Captain Arnold's

Wedding Chronicles

Confessions of a Wedding Officiant

Stories that will touch your heart, make you cry, and make you smile.

For couples getting married, For couples that are married. Even for those that are Divorced.

Captain Arnold Wonsever

(Interfaith Chaplain)

Copyright © 2023

All Rights Reserved

Disclaimer:

This is a work of nonfiction, and, as such, references will be made to true events, people, and places in the life and work of the author, Captain Arnold Wonsever. While all stories have been written from recollection, they have been retold in a way to present the information as accurately as possible. In order to protect the identities of persons described in this book, all names, dates, and images have been changed or altered.

Dedication

For Sheila

My Wife of 66 Wonderful Years

And Still Counting!

Acknowledgment

I would like to thank the thousands of couples whose wedding ceremony I had the pleasure and honor of performing, perhaps some of them are in this book and would like to say to them once again the following:

"Treat yourselves and each other with respect and remind yourselves often of what brought you together. Give the highest priority to the tenderness, gentleness, and kindness that your connection deserves. When frustration, difficulty and fear assail your relationship – as they threaten all relationships at one time or another – remember always to focus on what is right between you, not only the part which seems wrong. In this way, you can always ride out the storms when clouds hide the face of the sun in your lives – always remembering that even if you lose sight of it for a moment, that sun is still there. And if each of you takes responsibility for the quality of your life together, it will be marked by abundance and delight. And you can take that to the bank! "May the spirit of love be ever a part of your lives so that the union we here celebrate this day be worthy of continued celebration tomorrow and tomorrow and tomorrow."

Benediction & Blessing

"Most gracious G-d: We thank you for the beauty of this moment. Send your richest blessing upon Jack and Mary whom we bless in your name, that they may love, honor, and cherish each other, amid the ever-changing scenes of this life. Look favorably upon them, that their home may be a haven of blessing and a place of peace. Grant them the fullness of years and guide them by the wise counsel of your word, and when their earthly life is complete, give them entrance into your everlasting kingdom. **And now…May G-d bless you and keep you. May G-d's presence shine upon you and be gracious to you, May G-d's presence be with you and give you peace always. Amen**

Before these witnesses and in keeping with ancient custom, Jack and Mary joined hands, stated their vows to each other and exchanged rings. Now, by the power and authority vested in me and according to the form of solemnization of marriage by the state of New York, but most of all by the power of your own love, It is with great pleasure and a privilege that I pronounce you husband and wife.

Congratulations! You may kiss your bride for as long as you like!"

An extra special thanks to my wife Sheila for lovingly supporting me throughout my journey in writing "The Wedding

Chronicles". Much gratitude and love to my daughters and their husbands, Donna and John and Lisa and Rich, who were there to help me every step of the way.

And to my beautiful granddaughters Nicole, Danielle and Alyssa and my grandson Jamie, all of you will always be my sun, moon, and stars.

I would like to acknowledge these individuals that have played significant roles in my life, contributing to my happiness and success in various ways. They deserve my sincere gratitude for their unwavering support and the positive impact they've had on my journey as a wedding officiant.

Capt. Pete S, Owner of the Skyline Princess: His beautiful tri-level motor yacht, the Skyline Princess, has been the backdrop for many memorable wedding ceremonies that I have performed. His commitment to providing an unforgettable experience on the water has left a lasting impression.

Buck T, My computer genius: Buck T has been a reliable and invaluable friend, always ready to help you out whenever you encounter computer problems. His genius in solving these issues has been a true blessing, and his support has made a significant difference in my life.

Chef Rob G, Culinary Maestro: Chef Rob deserves special recognition for his exceptional culinary skills. His creations, whether it's delicious food or those mouthwatering desserts, have added an extra layer of delight to every cruise. His dedication to providing the best dining experiences at many of the weddings I have performed on the Skyline Princess is truly appreciated.

"A very special letter by a very special Grand daughter"

On April 17th, 2011, I performed a wedding ceremony for a beautiful couple at the historic "Inn at Woodstock Hill", a lovely spot on this planet that had it all. Romantic elegance, country charm, gracious ambiance and tranquil beauty, all nestled in the beautiful hills of Connecticut. And what even made it more special, is that with well close to two thousand wedding ceremonies that I've performed, I've known the Bride that stood before me since the day she was born. I've watched her grow into a beautiful young lady and shared many special days in her life. Oh! By the way, she's my Granddaughter! A few weeks later, she wrote me this note that I share with all my couples. And as a further update, I have been blessed by becoming a Great Grandfather to her beautiful daughter "Clara", who is the apple of my eye and the sunshine in my life!

Dear Grandpa,

When we decided to get married, we knew the true heart and focus for us would be the ceremony. Initially, I felt so honestly overwhelmed by so much of what we laughingly called the "wedding industrial complex" and all the unnecessary distractions and drama that wedding planning unfortunately but inevitably brings. We wanted to stay with the true meaning of the day. We wanted words that merged our two lives and brought eternal symbols and rituals to life in a solemn, but joyous way. We wanted something simple, elegant, and deeply meaningful. And that is exactly what you provided.

As a writer and teacher, I searched through many, many stacks of books trying to find the right words to pledge a lifetime to another person. You told me you had it all set and ready, and not to worry or stress. Finally, I had the faith to believe you and trust your experience and drop my intimidating task. After all, I had seen you perform ceremonies for other couples and each time was wonderful and flawless. I put my books away and left it up to you. I'm glad I did. Your ceremony is just the right balance of humorous and sentimental. It is exactly on the mark.

The funny thing is, many of the words spoken were exactly some of the things I stumbled across and loved the very most. Certain lines of poems and sayings that were exactly what I had found and underlined were weaved together with a masterful touch. It's really as though you read our minds and found the wise words about the sacred commitment and unparalleled love marriage brings. You did all the work finding the right words so we could simply focus on the experience itself. I am so grateful for that.

You said everything we wanted you to say and much more. Your engaging, rich voice and touching sentiments brought tears of emotion to guests we know well and even to strangers witnessing the truth and beauty of your words. To listen to you speak about love is transformative and resonates with every person present. We were so touched and moved by the magic of your ceremony and so was everyone joining us in a perfect moment of connection and bliss.

We have and we will reflect back often to the meaningful words spoken and revel in the powerful and transformative ceremony you created. You helped us focus on the true purpose of the day: to connect our lives and pause to be grateful and celebrate the love that holds our families together.

Love Always,

Nicole and Josh

Table of Contents

Dedication iv

Acknowledgment v

"A very special letter by a very special ix

Grand daughter" ix

PREFACE xiv

A Beautiful Ending that I Made Happen. 1

With Just a Little Touch of Spanish 5

Better Late Than Never 11

Feelings from a Bride That Will Touch Your Heart 16

Getting Married in a Cemetery, Part I 30

Getting Married in a Cemetery, Part II 33

Getting Married in a Cemetery, Part III 36

The Captain's Ceremony with a Touch of Hawaii 39

My Beautiful Cruise Ship Weddings 43

It Was Heard Around the World 66

It Just Had To Be on the Queen Mary II 68

They Found Love at a Citgo Gas Station 73

Up, Up and Away! 80

Till Death Do Us Part 85

An Accident That Saved Her Life 91

A Million-Dollar Wedding 95

A Surprise Wedding with Some Jail House Blues! 113

Valentine's Day at Times Square, What a Crowd! 145

The Great Train Wedding 165

I'm in the New York Times Check the Video! 173

The Wedding without a Bride & Groom (almost...) 186

Questions and Answers 190

About The Author 199

PREFACE

ABOUT THE CAPTAIN…

For more than 48 years, Captain Arnold has been an active Captain licensed by the United States Coast Guard to operate or navigate passenger-carrying vessels. He is also the only Captain that is an ordained chaplain registered with the City Clerk's Office of the City of New York. He has performed beautiful, unique, and memorable wedding ceremonies on land, at sea and in the air, aboard many major cruise ships of the wedding couple's choice or reception facility of their choice.

His amazing Wedding Ceremony of Love has been seen and heard worldwide and continues to receive rave reviews from those couples that have experienced his amazing wedding ceremony. He has performed his ceremony before hundreds of couples on the iconic Red Steps at Times Square, NYC, on Valentine's Day for two consecutive years, having been requested directly by the Times Square Alliance to perform a mass Vow Renewal ceremony streamed live worldwide.

He has also been selected to perform the first-ever two-minute flash wedding ceremony on ABC's Good Morning America before 6 million viewers.

The New York Times wrote, "Hollywood gave a big boost to the myth that captains could legally join couples on the open seas. In New York, Captain Arnold, an ordained Chaplain, is making this myth a reality". A personal interview with Captain Arnold now appears on the New York Times digital website and can be seen by typing "A Marriage at Sea? Get Me Rewrite" into your web browser.

He has been Voted "Best of Weddings" by couples of The Knot, Wedding Wire, and LI Wedding Brides, and further assists couples in personalizing their vows that highlight the sentiments and emotions of their most important day.

While his specialties are non-denominational, interfaith, interracial, and LGBTQ weddings, he has performed many second marriages and anniversary celebrations with re-affirming vows. As a recently retired exclusive wedding officiant for many of the major cruise ships in the New York tri-state area, such as Norwegian, Princess, Celebrity, Carnival, Disney and Royal Caribbean cruise lines, many families and their guests will remember for many years to come the amazing wedding ceremonies that he has performed for them aboard these ships. Yes, of course, he has had the pleasure and experience of giving many couples the perfect wedding ceremony that their families and guests will remember for many years to come; several of them are in this book. I hope you enjoy this book as much as he did while writing it. You can let him know at captarnold@gmail.com. By the way, he still performs weddings in the NY, CT, and NJ areas. Maybe he will see you at a wedding ceremony that he will be performing at one day!

It could even be yours!

WEDDING CHRONICLES

A Beautiful Ending that I Made Happen.

While living in Florida, I received a call from Karla, an excellent former manager of the Skyline Princess, a beautiful dinner cruise charter yacht that sails out of the World's Fair Marina in Flushing, New York.

"Can you perform a ceremony on the Saturday of Memorial Day Weekend?" she asked.

"Of course," I replied after checking my schedule. Immediately I planned arrangements for my flight, car rental, and overnight accommodation.

It was a miserable, rainy day when I arrived. The plane was late, and no cars were available. I had to wait two hours, and traffic was bumper to bumper. Would I get to the boat on time? Either way, they knew I was coming and weren't going anywhere without me!

When I finally arrived at the Marina, I noticed everyone was already seated and waiting for the ceremony to start. I met the bride, Ann, and the groom, Lenny, in the bridal suite and began to ask some of my usual questions so as to customize my ceremony. I wanted to add that personal touch that would reflect their feelings for each other and anything they might want to mention during the proceedings.

Ann was Puerto Rican and had lived in Puerto Rico most of

her life. Lenny was a Jewish boy from New York whose job took him to Puerto Rico from time to time. It was on one of his business trips that he met and fell in love with Ann.

But that was just the start of their story. During my conversations with them, they asked me to say something nice about Nancy, Lenny's grandmother. They said that she had always supported their love for each other and was always there for them during their courtship. The emphasis on Nancy's support made it plain to see that the relationship between Ann and Lenny was not totally accepted in Lenny's family.

Many interfaith marriages have a happy ending, but there are some that don't. I wanted this one to have a happy beginning, so I probed a little more and learned that Lenny's mother was currently seated amongst the guests. She was originally going to walk her son down the aisle but then changed her mind for reasons that led me to believe she was against this interfaith marriage from the start.

"Show me where his mom is sitting," I instructed Karla. I approached his mother and asked if I could have a few words with her in private.

We walked into the wheelhouse, and then I said, "I know how you feel, and I want you to know that you are not alone in your feelings. There are always those who will never approve of interfaith marriage and will use every obstacle they can think of to try and prevent it from happening.

"But it's not about those people, and it's not about your feelings today. Today is about them - your son and his future wife. It's his happiness that's what's most important, not yours. It's his life we are talking about, not yours.

"You're his mom, and you love him. You raised him to be a fine young man. You've made many sacrifices for him; now, on the most important day of his life, you abandon him. I want you to think ahead. Ann and Lenny will have children one day, and you will be a grandmother. Don't you want to hold your grandchild and love him like you did with your son?

"Be happy today! Erase those feelings you've kept inside you and join your son and his bride. Show them your love and support for their happiness and the new life they're about to share together. If you don't, you'll look back on this day and regret it for the rest of your life."

Her eyes welled up with tears, and as soon as she walked back to her seat, she was surrounded by other relatives and friends. I could see they were asking her questions from both sides, but she didn't reply. She just sat still, lost deep in her thoughts.

I walked back into the bridal suite. There were only a few minutes to go before showtime, and I still needed to check about the rings and the marriage license. A knock on the door interrupted us, but it was a welcome interruption. It was Lenny's mom.

She looked at her son and then at Anna. "Forgive me," she said. "I love you both and want you to be happy."

With those words, she rushed to them and hugged them. Tears came from every eye in the room, including mine. The ceremony went on, she walked her son down the aisle and smiled, and an atmosphere of beauty and love filled the air. It was a very happy time for all.

WEDDING CHRONICLES

With Just a Little Touch of Spanish

As soon as I first took the call from Joy, I knew that we were in the process of planning a very beautiful wedding. I arranged to meet Joy and her mom at a little café in New York to discuss all the little details, and from the start, there were a few important things they wanted to bring to my attention.

Joy herself was Peruvian and Jewish. Her fiancé, Ernesto, was from Spain. Both worked for the United Nations - Joy in New York and Ernesto in Paris. The wedding itself would take place in New York, with the reception to be held at the very beautiful Penn Club in New York City.

Ernesto planned to take 10 days off from his Paris post to New York for the wedding. Approximately 18 of his family and friends (none of which spoke a word of English) would also fly in for the occasion.

Knowing that there may be somewhat of a language barrier, I suggested early in our meeting that it would be a good idea to think about interpreting the ceremony from English to Spanish. This would allow those that did not understand English well to be able to better enjoy the ceremony.

Needless to say, the wheels began to turn in Joy's pretty little head and, low and behold, enter Manny Renna, an official U.S. interpreter, for the ceremony.

CAPTAIN ARNOLD WONSEVER

I met Manny, Joy, and Ernesto the Monday before the wedding. After some discussion, it was decided that Manny would stand behind Ernesto's family and friends, repeating various segments of my ceremony in Spanish for the entire group to hear. With full interpretation, the ceremony would now take twice as long.

When the night of the wedding came on March 5, 2004, plans changed, and it was decided that only the vows and the wedding ring ceremony would be interpreted in Spanish. Manny would be seated near me, and at the appropriate time, I would introduce him for the interpretation.

That evening, however, Manny approached me, looking pale, worried, and somewhat frightened.

"What's wrong, Manny?" I asked. "You look sick!"

"Captain," he replied, "I've done interpretations for the President's State of the Union Address, for many of the National Security Sessions, and for just about every important U.N. Assembly event, but I've never done a wedding!"

I laughed and assured him all would be well.

As expected, the ceremony went beautifully, to say the least. Sometime during cocktail hour, I saw Manny running toward me, hand outstretched to shake mine.

"You were right, Captain," he said. "Do you have anything more for me to do?"

As of that day, Manny became my official U.S. Spanish interpreter.

As for Ernesto and Joy, the happy couple moved shortly thereafter to their home in Paris, promising to keep in touch. They also sent me a beautiful letter of gratitude that I'm happy to share with you in the letter below.

CAPTAIN ARNOLD WONSEVER

International Institute for Educational Planning

Institut International de Planification de l'Education

Paris, 19 May 2004

Dear Captain Arnold,

It's been two months since we got married in New York City. Now, living in Paris, we look back to this special day with joy and happiness. Our wedding celebration was so special and precious to us. We remember the first meetings with you when we talked about how important the ceremony was to us. Your warmth from the very beginning and your caring personality made us realize that we had made the perfect choice in you.

All your words had a great impact not only on us but also on our guests. You conducted the ceremony with a masterful combination of poetic style, talented wordings, loving metaphors, and joyous wishes for our union. All this captivated everyone's attention, moved us in each one of the moments. The humorous parts were amusing and enjoyable too.

We have placed the vows that you generously presented us with, in a very special place in our home in Paris. We treasure our ceremony and know that you really made it special.

We wish you happiness, good health, and success. Hopefully, you will continue making other couples' unions as special and wonderful as you did with ours.

With our most sincere appreciation,

Joy & Ernesto

On a very happy note, I recently received an email in English and Spanish from my lovely couple telling me about the newest member of their family.

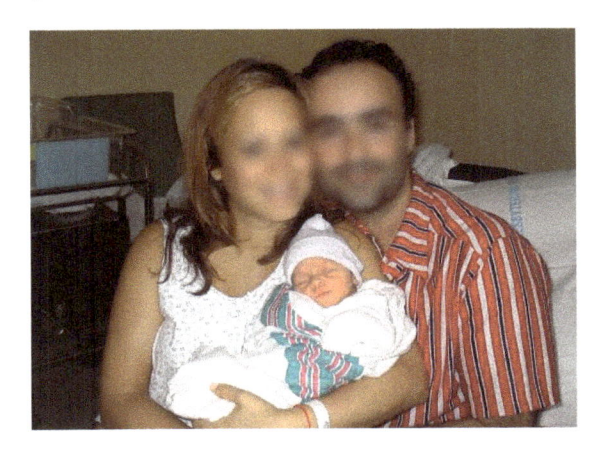

Dear Captain Arnold,

It is with great joy that we take the opportunity to announce the birth of our son, Andres, on 5 July 2006. Mom and baby are doing very well. We are now busy with the transition, sleepless nights and caring for

CAPTAIN ARNOLD WONSEVER

baby. Some pics are attached below (which would have needed several days of downloading to make individual emails separately for each one of you; our apology).

With love and best wishes for all,

Joy and Ernesto

WEDDING CHRONICLES

Better Late Than Never

It was one of those weddings where everything that could possibly go wrong did. The bride was over two hours late for her wedding, and the groom had forgotten their license.

I've performed at weddings before where the timetable is moved up slightly due to traffic, or the bride, for whatever reason, seems to need some extra time for those "little things," but I'm really talking about minutes.

Ten, fifteen, or even thirty minutes is acceptable, but when a bride and all of her bridesmaids are over two hours late, it makes you wonder. How and why would this ever happen, especially when the wedding was to take place on a yacht with a total contracted time of only four hours?

Eddy and Mary were to be married on the Nautical Princess, a great-looking yacht that sails out of Freeport, Long Island, in New York. For this wedding, the boarding time was scheduled for 4:15 pm, with a 4:30 pm ceremony to start promptly.

Prior to boarding, I asked Eddy for the wedding license as I always like to check and see that everything is in order, prepare the witnesses, and show them where they will be signing.

"Dad, do you have the license?" Eddy shouted out to his father.

"No," his father replied, "I think your brother has it."

We then went hunting for his brother, only to find out that he didn't have it either.

"So, where is the license, Eddy?" I asked.

He paused for a moment, taking the time to think until he came to the final shocking realization. "Oh my God! I left it at home on the kitchen table...and the kitchen table just happens to be in Manhattan!"

"Well, then," I said, "if that's the case, I can't marry you."

On that note, I was immediately capsized by not one, not two, not even three people, but several guests (including cousins and uncles) that were all pleading with me to perform the ceremony and promising that the license would be in my hands by tomorrow morning.

"Look," I said, "here's what I'm going to do. I'll perform the ceremony, but it won't be legal until I complete and mail in the license to the marriage license bureau."

It was then agreed upon that I would do a "mock" marriage ceremony (or, for lack of a better word, a "symbolic" ceremony) and that on the following morning, before 10 am, Eddy would come by my home for another five-minute ceremony and give me the license.

The time was now 4:30 and the bride, Mary, had not yet

arrived. Five o'clock came, and still no bride. Eddy was now getting a little worried, and as I looked out of the window from the boat, I could see Eddy pacing up and down outside.

The guests were soon seated, and everyone was wondering what was going on. At 5:45 pm, there was still no sign of the bride, and Eddy thought he'd lost her for sure. I insisted that the staff begin serving some hors d'oeuvres and drinks to keep the guests from abandoning the ship.

At about 6 pm, they were finally able to contact the bride by cell phone and learn what went wrong. After nearly two hours had passed, it was a stupid blunder on the part of the limo driver. He had been taking them to Montauk instead of Freeport.

As luck would have it, they were in Lindenhurst when they realized that they were heading in the wrong direction. They turned around and were given directions by the staff at the yacht (and just in case you were wondering, the limo company did reimburse them for a portion of their wedding cruise).

Finally, the bride arrived with her entourage of bridesmaids (four to be exact), and the ceremony began about two hours and thirty minutes after it was scheduled.

Eddy had been outside alone, pacing up and down and very concerned as to why his bride had not yet arrived. All this time waiting and not knowing what to think was killing him.

When the word finally came through that it was an error on the part of the limo driver, he felt somewhat relieved, knowing that his bride was okay and that no accidents or disasters of any sort had occurred.

When he knew that the limo was close, it was then that he boarded the yacht to stand beside me and wait for his bride to arrive. As the limo pulled up, Eddy looked out the window and saw Mary.

From that moment on, he found it difficult to compose himself, and his eyes welled up with tears. He cried during the ceremony, and I had to stop every now and then so he could take a deep breath and wipe his eyes.

He was very emotional, and I, for one, could understand why. The thoughts that must have gone through Eddy's mind during that waiting period must have been a nightmare for him.

Much later, at 2 am, my phone rang while I was in a dead sleep.

"Hello?" I responded, shivering.

Our concierge answered. "Captain, this is Sam," he said. "I have a young man here who says he has something for you."

"You have the wrong number!" I snapped, hanging up the phone.

Again, it rang. "Hello, Captain. This is Eddy. I have the license."

After he repeated it a few times, I realized what was happening. "Eddy," I said, "stay right there. I'll be down in a few minutes."

They were going to Columbia for their honeymoon, and since they had a very early flight, they thought it would best to drop by on the way to the airport to drop off the license.

I met them in the lobby, looked over the license, said a few words, and then again said, "You may kiss your bride."

"Now everything's nice and legal," I told them. "Enjoy your honeymoon!"

I then got into the elevator with my eyes half closed, entered my apartment, and went to sleep with the license in my hand.

CAPTAIN ARNOLD WONSEVER

Feelings from a Bride That Will Touch Your Heart

In 2004, Captains couldn't perform a wedding ceremony as it was required that they be legally ordained ministers in addition to being registered with the city clerk's office of the City of New York.

A minister, or wedding officiant as they were also called, needed to be recognized as one that could legally perform a marriage in a specific jurisdiction, be it a town, a village, or a city in New York, New Jersey, or Connecticut.

The year before, I lived in Florida and performed many weddings on many of the luxury boats that made their home port there. To perform a ceremony in Florida, you only needed to become a Notary Public.

But by this time, I had plenty of motor yacht weddings all "locked up," you might say, because I met all the qualifications that were required and recognized in every state.

It was just the right time, too, because yacht weddings were beginning to get very popular in New York in particular. One of the first things a couple would ask is if a Captain could marry them. As this question was previously met with a resounding "no," you can imagine the disappointment. This disappointment, however, would soon come to an end.

When my wife and I decided to move back to New York,

many of the motor yachts could now tell their couples that they had a Captain to legally perform their wedding ceremony. I, therefore, became busy, very busy, and didn't even have a website at the time. It was all happening by word of mouth and referrals.

Along the way, another wonderful opportunity opened for me where I became not only the exclusive wedding officiant but also orchestrated beautiful weddings for some of the major cruise ships that sailed from the New York tri-state area, like the Royal Caribbean, Norwegian, Celebrity and Princess Cruise Lines, to name a few. But that is another story for another time.

I'm sharing this history with you because the story I'm about to tell involves a somewhat unique wedding that took place on a beautiful boat.

It involves a very special bride that touched my heart, and I hope her story will touch yours as well.

It was mid-afternoon on April 10, 2004, and I was getting ready to leave for a wedding ceremony that I was going to perform aboard the beautiful Nautical Princess, a luxurious motor yacht that sails out of Freeport, Long Island.

I had my hand on the doorknob, ready to walk out of my apartment, when the phone rang. My wife answered it and called out to me, shouting, "It's RJ from the Nautical Princess! He needs to talk with you."

RJ was one of the managers in the office that referred couples to me. He wasn't the only one as it was a large operation and also included the staff of another beautiful paddle wheel river boat called the Nautical Belle.

"What's up, RJ?" I asked. "Is there anything I need to know about tonight's wedding?"

I usually like to arrive at a wedding about 45 minutes to an hour before a ceremony so that I can have some personal words with my couple, take care of the paperwork, see their rings, and give them a quick run-through of what they can expect. I simply tell them to let me be the director and producer of their special day, and they'll love it.

It's important to connect with a couple and make them feel comfortable and relaxed before, during, and after the ceremony, and I have all the right ingredients to do just that. I also have a small table with a wine glass of ice water and a package of Kleenex tissues on it in case the bride or groom cries. Many do.

"No," RJ said. "Everything is fine. I'll see you when you arrive, but I have a big favor to ask of you."

"Sure thing," I replied. What can I do for you?"

"You know you're doing a ceremony for Doris and Robert next week on the Princess. Well, Doris called me earlier this morning and said she would really like to speak with you ASAP."

"I don't understand. I spoke to her all about my ceremony when she retained me. I went over every detail and answered any questions and concerns she had.

I told her that I'd be calling her the week of her wedding to review the bride and groom checklist.

"We'll go over any last-minute details she'd like to talk about then," I assured him. "Did she say why she needed to speak with me in person and not on the phone?"

"No; to be honest, I have no idea why she wants to talk with you in person," he said, "but I can tell you that she insisted. And by the tone in her voice, I think you should.

"Look, she lives right here in Freeport, only about 10 minutes from the boat. Why don't you stop by before coming here and spend a little time with her to find out what she wants?"

"O.K., RJ. Give her a call for me and tell her I'll be there at about 4 PM. That will give me about an hour to spend with her. I'll get to the bottom of it and let you know what all this urgency is about when I see you later."

"Done."

I had Doris's address on my information form, so I pumped it into my hand-held Garmin GPS. I had an idea where she lived in

Freeport, but to be honest, I trusted my GPS more than my memory. I also had a lot on my mind, what with this bride insisting on talking to me when I had another ceremony to perform in a few hours.

I parked my car right in front of her home, knocked on her door, and soon enough heard children's voices calling out: "Ma, the Captain is here! Ma, the Captain is here!!"

The door opened, and that was the first time I came eye-to-eye with Doris and her three adorable and very young children. Doris herself looked very young for a bride - very thin, with sky-blue eyes and a pretty face framed with long blonde hair.

"Come in, Captain," she said warmly, "please have a seat in the dining room. I'm just finishing up making a pot of coffee. Would you like a cup?"

"Sure," I thought to myself, "I have an hour to spend."

On that note, she ushered her kids into the playroom and asked them to stay there as she had a few things she had to go over with me about the wedding. Their reaction to the word "wedding" was all I needed to be sure of their excitement over it.

Doris then came into the dining room with two cups of coffee in her hand, handed me one, and sat down at the other end of the table. "Captain," she said, "I can't thank you enough for coming, and I really appreciate it very much. I know you have a wedding to perform later, but I felt that I needed to speak with you before our ceremony so you'd have all the details beforehand about Robert and me."

She had a beautiful voice and spoke with a kind of authority…and my curiosity was killing me. In my mind, I was thinking, "Why now? What could be so important?"

A few seconds had passed, and she seemed to have taken a deep breath. With somewhat of a half-smile, she simply stated: "Captain, I'm marrying my husband's brother."

I was stunned. My mind went blank since I wasn't sure I'd heard her right. She's marrying her husband's brother. How could this be? But I could see it wasn't a joke when she said that, and a sigh of relief came over her as though a heavy weight had been lifted from her shoulders.

"I know," she said. "I know it probably comes as a shock to you as it has to many, but you're the one person that's going to marry us, that will unite us together for the rest of our lives. I needed you to know everything about this situation and why it came about.

"I just couldn't tell you when I retained your services. I thought I would wait until we got closer to our wedding day. No one at the boat knows about this, not even RJ, but when he told me such wonderful things about you, and then when we spoke on the phone, I knew I'd made the right decision in retaining you. I consider you the most important person at this wedding and wanted to open my heart to you now. May I explain it to you?"

"Of course!" I replied.

"You see, Captain, my husband, who I loved with all my heart and with whom I shared a wonderful life, was killed in the 9/11 attack on the World Trade Center. He worked there at the time when that tragedy happened.

"When I learned of it, I was devastated. I felt the world had caved in on me. I had my children and now had only precious memories of us all together as a family that were never to be anymore. These were truly the darkest hours of my life. No one and I mean no one, had the compassion, the love, and the understanding that I needed to survive this terrible nightmare I was living in except one person. That one person was my husband's brother, Robert.

"It was Robert that came to me in my darkest hour to console me, be with me and save me from a hell that no one should experience. I know that thousands of families suffered terribly from this tragedy, and I feel for each and every one of them. But when it hits home, in your heart, you can't help but think, what now? What will happen to me? What will happen to my children, and who will take care of us? I'm afraid, so afraid. What will I do, what can I do?

"Enter Robert again and again he made me feel secure in the knowledge that he would always be there for me and my children every step of the way. He was my salvation and my knight in shining armor. The kids knew that Daddy wasn't coming home anymore and that Robert would be with us from now on. As young as they were, they accepted that, and in their own way, I think they understood why.

"Robert was married, but he was not happy. It was an unhappy marriage almost to begin with, and both he and his wife knew it and felt it. They'd felt the same way towards each other, like two strangers living together. It was unhappy time for them even long before 9/11 happened, and when it did happen, Robert was drawn to me, being there for me. Creating just another reason for his marriage to finally come to an end by divorce.

"This was the beginning of a new life for him, one that no one would ever have thought would unfold as it did for the both of us. You see, Captain, we fell in love and in a very strange way, and people who know us say it was fate. But I think God brought us together to be happy again and live our lives as they were meant to be."

After listening to Doris for a while, I could feel her love and admiration for this man and couldn't help but agree that God had played a major role in this union.

Our discussion turned to the wedding day, and no question about it, I could see she was very excited. "As you know, Captain," she said, "it's not going to be a big wedding. We will only have about 17 or 18 guests. Only those very close to us who understand what we went through will attend. Some, even members of our own family, are not coming because they feel differently about us being together.

"I can respect that, but if they were in my shoes, I don't think they'd feel the same way. It's more important for me and my children to be happy than to have to worry about what others may feel about my wedding day."

We spoke about the ceremony, and I explained how it would flow and what the vows were like. Typically, at the beginning of my ceremony, I pay tribute to loved ones that can't be present. They may be too ill or may have passed on. The events of this day would normally not be complete without taking a moment to remember these loved ones. In this situation, however, I thought it would create some strong emotions, so I suggested leaving it out. She agreed.

As I finished my coffee, I said to Doris, "I'm happy that you called RJ and told him you wanted to speak with me. I certainly can see why this was so important to you, and I can promise you will love my ceremony because my words will be exactly what you'll want to hear."

She walked me to the door but first called out to the children to say goodbye. She gave me a hug and thanked me repeatedly for coming to see her.

I then got into my car and headed straight to the Nautical Princess to perform my 6 o'clock wedding ceremony. It was perfect.

RJ came onto the ship just before I was getting ready to leave to ask me about my meeting with Doris.

"It's late," I told him. "I'll stop by during the week and tell you all about it. I think you'll be impressed, and I know you'll be surprised." And I left with a smile on my face.

The week passed quickly, and April 17th, 2004, was Doris and Robert's wedding day. It almost seemed like yesterday that I was at her home, speaking to her about all the events that had led up to that day.

Her children were dressed beautifully, and I could see they were still very excited, as most children are when I perform at a wedding.

But this one felt different. It felt like I was about to unite a family for the rest of their lives like in no other wedding I'd performed before. I even felt special about this day.

Finally, the ceremony began. When it came time for them to say their vows to each other, I said, "Robert, Doris, I want you to face each other now. Hold hands and look into each other's eyes because you are about to repeat those words that will bind you together for the rest of your lives."

They did just that. I could feel how they put every fiber of their being into the words, but before I could speak again, Doris turned to me.

"Captain," she said, "can I say just a few words to Robert?"

"Of course, you can."

Doris then took out a piece of paper that was folded in her left hand, unfolded it, and glanced down at it for just a moment. She said the following to Robert without ever reading or looking at the paper again. I could tell it came from her heart.

"Robert, I am looking at you and can hardly believe what my eyes see or what my heart tells me. You came to me unselfishly as my unexpected salvation, bearing pain all your own in your hungry and mournful soul, embracing mine with your soothing words and gentle caress.

"In our hearts beat a hopeful song we barely understood. Now, we are not afraid and are off on a hopeful journey long before we knew we could.

"I've asked myself, 'What if I never had you if your life hadn't unfolded as it had at the time? How did this come to be?' I'd never have this feeling in my heart; therefore, I know we were meant to be. You are part of my destiny.

"In these times of fear, prayer has so often proven vain, and hope seemed like the waning tide, too swiftly flown away. Yet now I'm standing here, my hearts so full, I can't explain, seeking faith and speaking words I never thought I'd say.

"Robert, I love you with all my heart. You've entered my soul, so sweet and so kind. In your arms, I always smile. You are my hero, baby. You have kept your word: that you would stand by me forever…

"I promise to love, honor and cherish you, and it is my conviction to make you feel loved every day for the rest of your life."

"Wow," I said to myself, looking around at their guests. There wasn't a dry eye on this boat; I must admit, even my eyes welled up. More Kleenex was used at this wedding than any other, and I don't think I'll ever see that again.

I looked at Robert and asked him if he'd like to say anything to Doris.

With tears running down his face and his voice breaking up, he said in a very shallow, low voice meant for her to hear, "I love you, Doris, with all my heart and soul. I will always be here for you and the kids; you can count on that." He leaned over and kissed her on her cheek.

When I declared them husband and wife at the end of the ceremony, I said, "Robert, you may kiss your bride for as long as you want." He did for about 15 seconds.

The celebration began as it does with all weddings. Hugs and kisses were exchanged with their guests while I waited by the bar, enjoying a few hors d'oeuvres and a Pepsi.

I waited until the guests wandered away from the couple to ask if they enjoyed my ceremony. Still with tears of joy in their eyes, they both hugged and thanked me before I started heading home.

As I was leaving, I turned around and walked back to Doris. "Would you mind if I have that beautiful note you held in your hand when you expressed your feelings to Robert?"

"Not at all," she said. She reached into her little purse, pulled out the note, and placed it in my hand. She placed both her hands around mine with a smile and said, "Maybe one day you'll write a book about some of the special weddings you do."

I left the boat that day with something to think about. Several weeks later, I received a note in the mail from Doris and Robert. The following is what She said.

WEDDING CHRONICLES

Dear Captain,

"...I would like to take this opportunity to thank you for assisting in creating a wonderful new memory for myself, Robert, and our family on our wedding day on the Nautical Princess in Freeport, NY.

Your caring nature and ability to create a uniquely warm and entertaining program for us throughout the evening made a perfect complement to our unique circumstances.

You turned an emotionally laden situation that I could've never imagined I'd find myself in into a lasting happy memory. I will always look back on this day in difficult times and smile. Your 'magic' is sure to last a lifetime for both Robert and I and our children.

Fondly,

Doris, Robert, David, Donny, and April"

They left New York shortly after, leaving behind those memories they chose not to remember, and now live in a beautiful small town in Maine. This is one wedding that I still think about from time to time. It really did touch my heart.

CAPTAIN ARNOLD WONSEVER

Getting Married in a Cemetery, Part I

It was around the end of April 2004 when I received a phone call from Marty. "Are you available to perform a ceremony on June 12th?" he asked.

I checked my schedule and replied that I was. I then asked where he would be getting married.

"In a cemetery," he calmly replied.

For a moment, I was stunned and needless to say; some weird thoughts went through my mind. "Why a cemetery?" I inquired. "Are your guests dying to come to see you? You're going to have a lot of deadheads and stiffs at your reception."

He laughed and then explained to me that his fiancée, Sheryl, was a "historic preservationist" and that she worked for the cemetery as an intern. Her job involved making tracings of many of the gravestones that were there from the Civil War and then writing a report on what it took to restore them.

"Hmmm…interesting," I thought. But he never told me where I would be standing while performing the ceremony.

June 12th finally arrived, and while driving to the cemetery, I couldn't help but think about where I was heading and where I would be standing. Would I be on a loved one's gravesite? Or perhaps in a mausoleum of some sort? Whew!! The suspense was killing me (no pun intended).

I finally arrived at the pearly gates (correction - the wrought iron gates) of the Greenwood Cemetery, a very famous cemetery where many famous people are buried. They even have walking tours!

"I'm here to perform a wedding ceremony," I said to the security officer at the gate. He looked at me with this weird kind of expression and then directed me to this magnificent and awesome-looking chapel. It was called "The Historical Chapel at the Greenwood Cemetery."

For a moment, I thought I was in Rome, London, or Paris, where such beautiful Gothic structures exist. When I stepped inside the chapel, I felt like I was in St. Patrick's Cathedral or a chapel that might very well be in the Vatical. Tiffany-stained glass surrounded me, and the architecture was truly extraordinary.

I was later told that this chapel was built by the same architects who built Grand Central Station. The chapel didn't have any state-of-the-art electronics, like a microphone or a speaker system, but it didn't need it. The acoustics were wonderful, and my voice projects rather well, so I really didn't need a microphone.

The ceremony started, and I could hear my voice as it resonated throughout the chapel. After the ceremony was over, I followed the couple as they walked toward the entrance.

CAPTAIN ARNOLD WONSEVER

While walking out, this sweet little old lady, still sitting in a pew on the aisle, grabbed my arm, looked up at me with tears in her eyes, and said, "You know, you sounded like God."

Getting Married in a Cemetery, Part II

Her Boss Found Me

Casey and Marge were at a party when they heard a woman say that she had attended a beautiful wedding ceremony in a cemetery. Even though they thought it was a little weird, they decided to check it out since they had not yet selected a location for their wedding.

They were quite surprised when they arrived at the cemetery and were directed to the chapel. They thought it was magnificent, and it took them but a second to say, "We love it; we'll take it" to the management staff at the cemetery.

June 1st would be their special day, and plans were set in motion to find a caterer, a florist, musicians and, most of all, the person who would marry them.

When they inquired at the management office of the cemetery if they could recommend someone, they were told no. The cemetery management office had never put my name on file because the previous weddings I had performed there resulted from couples finding and contacting me through my website.

Their subsequent search for a wedding officiant began, and many interviews with different clergy proved to be unsatisfying, leaving Casey and Marge feeling frustrated and disappointed.

While at work one day, Marge's boss saw how upset she was. Her wedding day was approaching, and she had yet to find an officiant. "Go back to your desk," her boss told her. "Relax awhile, grab a cup of coffee, and let me check around."

Her boss got on the computer and, as luck would have it, found my website. "Look what I found," he said. "I think you're going to love this!"

A little browsing around on my website revealed to her that I had performed the only two weddings that had ever been performed in the Greenwood Cemetery. She called me with bated breath, keeping her fingers crossed and hoping I was available. I was.

Before the wedding, we met in New York City at a lovely restaurant, chatted, and discussed the details over a delicious meal. The wedding was beautiful and very special. After all, how many people do you know were married in a cemetery?

WEDDING CHRONICLES

Getting Married in a Cemetery, Part III
It Almost Happened on the Brooklyn Bridge

Jane and Bob called me in July and asked if I was available to perform their ceremony on August 14th, 2004. I replied that I was and asked where they planned to marry.

"On the Brooklyn Bridge," they said.

I told them there would be tons of traffic and no place for guests to park. Additionally, the trucks that would be coming by would make a tremendous amount of noise, and what if it rained?

"Is there a "plan B?" I asked. "You wouldn't want to put your guests through the hassle of getting on the bridge in the first place."

Jane thought it over and said that I might be right. I gave them some time to think it over.

Two days passed, and Jane called to say they'd changed plans. They were getting married at a cemetery.

"Let me guess," I said with a smile, "the Greenwood Cemetery?"

"How did you know that?" she asked, a little surprised. "Are you also psychic?!"

I assured her that I was not psychic (even if I *am* also a

magician) and told her that I'd recently performed a ceremony there in June.

Jane had remembered playing on the beautiful grounds of the cemetery as a little girl. When she visited the chapel with Bob, both had taken one look at the place and knew it was where they wanted to be married. Having now been there a few times myself, I could tell them with a good amount of certainty that it was a place they wouldn't soon forget!

CAPTAIN ARNOLD WONSEVER

WEDDING CHRONICLES

The Captain's Ceremony with a Touch of Hawaii

As a Captain, I have performed many wedding ceremonies on luxurious yachts and large cruise ships like the QM-2. It never ceases to amaze me how beautiful these nautical events are. From the impeccably dressed, white-gloved, uniformed staff to those delicious delicacies served, you can't ask for anything more when it comes to a wedding reception.

But when I was asked by the *Ship Wedding Planners*, representatives of the Norwegian Cruise Line, to perform the 1st inaugural wedding ceremony aboard the Pride of America, I thought to myself that this was really the icing on the cake. It was indeed an honor and a privilege to be a part of such an event.

Jack and Betty were the 1st couples to be married aboard the Pride of America, the largest U.S. Flag cruise ship in history. It made its star-spangled debut on June 17th, 2005, in New York City. After much media hoopla and a series of inaugural festivities, complete with a christening ceremony that was held on Friday, June 17th, in the Big Apple, the Pride of America made her way to her homeport of Honolulu, Hawaii.

The Pride of America's all-American theme even extended to the ship's spacious public areas. However, the flavor was all Hawaiian on this special day, and I was asked to include a little "something" about Hawaiian tradition in this beautiful ceremony.

After a quick lesson in the Hawaiian language given to me by the Hawaiian ambassador, I was ready to perform my ceremony with a little touch of Hawaii in it. Here is an excerpt from my ceremony:

"The lei (a beautiful string of flowers) is the Hawaiian symbol of love and aloha. The custom of giving and receiving lies at weddings began in the days of old Hawaii.

"During the wedding ceremony, the minister bound the hands of the bride and groom as a symbol of the couple's commitment to each other. During the lei exchange, the following words were usually spoken: '**E lei kau, e lei ho'oilo i ke aloha.**' This meant 'love is worn like a wreath through the summers and winters; love is everlasting'."

The groom then presented his bride with a beautiful white lei that he placed around her neck, and the bride placed a colorful lei around the groom's neck.

WEDDING CHRONICLES

CAPTAIN ARNOLD WONSEVER

WEDDING CHRONICLES

My Beautiful Cruise Ship Weddings

Every now and then, for many of us throughout our lives, various opportunities knock on our door, and there comes a time when we must make a quick decision if we want to pursue them. Some are good, and some are not so good. These are some of the gambles we face in life if we want to get ahead instead of staying where we are. Many of us create our own opportunities from a dream or a great idea and then work hard to make it a reality.

The opportunity that presented itself to me in particular arrived by way of a phone call at 6 a.m. on the last Thursday in April of 2005. I like to think it was a "golden opportunity."

I picked up the phone immediately after the first ring. I didn't want my wife to wake up.

"Hello? Is this Captain Arnold?" a voice inquired.

"Yes," I replied, still somewhat in sleep mode. I usually say, "Hi, this is Captain Arnold. How may I help you?" This time the guy on the other end beat me to it.

"My name is Buck Peters, and I'm the purchasing agent and human resource manager for a company called '*Ship Wedding Planners*,' or 'SWP' for short. We're a Florida-based company responsible for booking and running all the weddings for just about every major cruise ship worldwide, or more specifically, at all locations where these ships make their home port. We also arrange weddings at sea, but that falls under another department of ours that I won't get into now."

"Why's he calling me?" I wondered to myself, "and why at this hour in the morning?"

Before I could say anything, he said, "We're doing a lot of business in the Northeast Corridor. Our busiest time for weddings is now while we're growing in areas of New York, New Jersey, and, on a more limited basis, at the Brooklyn Cruise Terminal."

Now I was beginning to get the reason for his call. I figured he must've been trying to sell me something, but it sounded interesting, and I felt for the moment that it was worthwhile listening to him. After all, this could possibly be my golden opportunity, and he might just open a whole new area of wedding ceremonies for me.

I didn't want to get ahead of myself just yet, however, so I let Buck continue to talk until I thought it was time for me to start asking some questions.

"We need someone to run the territory where we're seeing the largest growth in weddings taking place, and you were highly recommended to us from a reliable source in New York," Buck explained. "To be honest, we did our own due diligence on you and your company, reviewed your beautiful website, and I must say that our president was impressed with so many of the wonderful testimonials your couples have sent you.

"So, my question to you is: would you be interested in joining our company to take over and run our cruise ship weddings in the Northeast?"

I'd felt that this was coming. I asked Buck if he'd hold on while I took this call in my office (only about 25 feet from my bedroom).

"No problem," he replied.

I think he must've sensed that I was still in bed when he called. "*Who makes phone calls this early in the morning?*" I thought again to myself, though he could also have been calling from his home.

At any rate, it gave me a chance to go grab a glass of cold orange juice to really wake me up. I hoped that it would at least help me ask intelligent questions that would leave us both with a good feeling and result in a positive outcome for each of us.

Before I could speak, Buck quickly answered some of the questions I'd been planning to ask. He reassured me that it wouldn't be necessary to come to Florida at any time because everything they'd require of me could be done solely by email or phone (and, if necessary, express overnight mail, which rarely happens).

That would've been my first question, and I was happy to

hear such a favorable reply. I wasn't about to relocate or start traveling to Florida, so the fact that all could be accomplished by phone, email and mail made me happy.

I also informed him that I had a lot on my plate in New York. With so many weddings booked and some that would book shortly, I couldn't afford to have a conflict, and my land weddings had to come first.

"I fully understand," he said, "but these weddings usually take place starting at about 10 a.m., and you and your team can be off the ship by 2:30 p.m. In fact, you can probably leave by about 1 p.m. since your team can finish up with the reception. That really leaves you free to head to your land weddings shortly after."

I turned on my computer while he was talking, looked at my schedule and noticed that many of my ceremonies were in the evening, with only a few starting in the early afternoon. This still left me plenty of time to get to my next wedding.

I was beginning to think that this could work for me! I was more than satisfied that there didn't have to be any conflict with my weddings in New York.

I also emphasized to him the importance that my land weddings take precedence over any ship weddings. I made it clear that I was the preferred wedding officiant for a large number of land venues that referred me to their clientele. I couldn't jeopardize relationships that had taken me years to build.

He understood my position and convinced me that all would work out just fine. "If you find that there's a conflict with one of your land weddings and one of our ship weddings, just hire a minister to perform the wedding on the ship. It's that simple, and believe me when I tell you that there are many ministers out there that would love to perform a wedding on a cruise ship."

This was just getting better and better, and Buck made it look like it was really easy to run these weddings. For the moment, I was starting to feel that this association could really work. It would open up a whole new revenue stream for me as well as connect me with some of the largest and most popular cruise ships in the industry.

Before New York and New Jersey came along, much of the public had always thought you had to go to Florida to sail on a cruise ship. This was no longer the case.

All I needed now was some good planning. I'd keep a record of all weddings coming up and treat the cruise ship weddings as a separate entity. I'd make sure that a conflict would never exist and wouldn't result in a couple being left standing at the altar with no wedding officiant to perform their ceremony.

"Installing certain safeguards is all that's needed, and that's an easy system to create," I said to myself.

I then asked Buck a question to which I thought I had the right to know the answer. "What happened to the people or company you were dealing with that handled these East Coast weddings before? Are they still involved, and why are you making this change?"

"No, we had to cut our relations with them. They just didn't work out. There were too many things they were involved with, and they just could not provide us with the services we'd expected. There was also a serious lack of communication between us and the people they'd used to service our couples and their guests. They were not the professionals we needed."

"To be honest, this was a bad reflection on us as well as some of the crew members on the ships that handled our weddings. We communicated with these ship crew members almost daily, and they finally told us it was time to make a change.

"We're looking for someone to take charge of our weddings in what has become an important part of our business in the New York tri-state market," he said. "That's why I contacted you."

I could sense that Buck was honest about the problems they were having, and he'd really explained it in a way that made sense. I understood the problem and agreed that the only way to change the way things were being handled was to get rid of the old and bring in the new.

WEDDING CHRONICLES

With the experience and background that I had in the wedding business, I felt that this was a situation that I could easily handle while at the same time providing a valuable service to his wedding couples and their guests. After all, one of the most important days in their lives would be their wedding day.

After listening to Buck explain a little more of the logistics of weddings on cruise ships, I finally said, "OK, Buck, I'm in. So, what's the next step? When's the next wedding coming up, and what do you need me to do now?"

I could hear Buck's sigh of relief. After a short pause, he said, "This Saturday, we have a wedding on a ship called the NCL Crown leaving from pier 90 at the Port of New York. That's a Norwegian Cruise Line ship, by the way." He added the last to make sure I knew what "NCL" stood for.

"Saturday?!" I echoed back. "Are you kidding? Today's Thursday! That's only two days away. I'm a one-man operation. I don't have any staff to bring, and I have no idea what I need to do when I get to the ship. Look, Buck, I'm a fast learner, but you're talking to me like I've been doing this for years."

Now I could hear Buck laugh. If I had him on Skype, I would probably have seen him with a big smile. "Don't worry, Captain," he said calmly. "I've got you covered."

"I'm having two of my best ship coordinators fly up to New

York tomorrow. They will meet you at the ship terminal to assist you with this wedding. These gals work at all the weddings here in Miami and Fort Lauderdale and know the business inside and out.

"You'll have the best teacher's right by your side, and I'm sure you'll find them very helpful. One of the coordinators even has a brother living on Long Island, and his daughter and her friend will also join you."

He further explained that the number of coordinators required was dependent on the number of guests at a wedding. "The ships suggest that for every 25 guests (including the bride and groom), we have 1 coordinator. This is included in any of the wedding packages that are purchased by the couple. If you have 50, you need 2 coordinators, 51 to 75, 3 coordinators, and so on.

"This will give you some idea as to the number of team members you will need to assign to these weddings when we send you our 'Final Wedding Report' (or 'FWR' for short)."

I suggested that he send me some samples of the paperwork that would be used. I wanted to review them to see if I needed him to designate someone on his staff to work with me and clarify things if it was necessary.

Buck informed me that he'd already designated someone by the name of Ralph to be my right hand all the way from Florida. Ralph had strict orders to give me top priority if I required any help.

WEDDING CHRONICLES

I mentioned how it would also be very comforting to have a direct line to their office until I got the hang of it and felt independent enough not to have to rely on contacting them all the time. After all, this was short notice for a big event, and I could see that there would probably be many more in the future.

Saturday arrived faster than I would've liked. As I drove into the city, I thought ahead about this event, picturing in my mind what a cruise ship wedding must look like in comparison to some of the land weddings I'd performed.

With a land wedding, I simply arrived at the location of the venue about 30 minutes prior to the ceremony, talked to the couple, completed the marriage license signing, performed my ceremony, and sometimes I'd stick around a little while to enjoy the smorgasbord cuisine the couple usually invites me to savor. I didn't expect that to happen on a cruise ship wedding, at least not yet.

I arrived at pier 90 in New York City, which was located at 12th Avenue and 49th Street. It was an older ship terminal, so it wasn't anything fancy. In fact, at that point, it looked a little run-down, like an old, big, very long building extending into the waters of the Hudson River. I was told that they were refurbishing a newer, fancier building close by that would be called Pier 88, but it wouldn't be ready for several years.

Since it's always too tough to find any parking in the streets in that area, I went right to the parking lot located at the top of their terminal. This lot on the roof was used as their primary parking area for passengers that drove into the city and needed to park their cars before boarding neighboring ships. The terminal made finding their cars after cruises more convenient.

As soon as I arrived, I found my way to the nearest coffee shop. I'd come a little earlier to check out some of the terminal areas before meeting with the coordinators scheduled to be there at 9:30 a.m.

The beautiful Norwegian Crown ship was already docked, and they were disembarking their passengers just as new passengers were beginning to file in to the terminal for their 7-day cruise. There were certainly lots and lots of people.

I sat at a table near the check-in area to be sure I would easily be found by the team coming from Florida. Just at 9:30 on the button, the coordinators walked into the terminal and headed straight for me.

I guess it must have been my uniform. The four gold stripes I wear on my sleeve can be seen from 100 feet away.

They were also wearing what you'd consider uniforms - black slacks, a black blazer or jacket, a white shirt, low black shoes, and no heels. They also had a gold pin on the left side of their jackets that read "Wedding Coordinator." It was very sharp and

WEDDING CHRONICLES

professional-looking indeed.

After a quick introduction, Maria, the "lead" coordinator, joined by Sandy, her assistant, and Jennifer and Rachel, the two girls living on Long Island, shook hands with me.

"Buck thinks very highly of you after you had that lengthy conversation with him this past Thursday," Maria said. "He thinks you'll be just great for these weddings."

"Thanks for the compliment," I replied. "I'm looking forward to working with you."

"I brought you a manual that covers just about everything concerning cruise ship weddings," she said. "It's provided to all the people who service our ships around the globe. It's what we'd call our 'bible.'

"I'll take you through everything, step by step, so you'll really know how we orchestrate cruise ship weddings once you review it. There are also several CDs of wedding music included, and I'll go over that with you once we're on the ship."

She told me that, in a few minutes, the wedding couple and their guests would start arriving at the terminal, and many would be coming from different directions. One of the most important things that needed to be done was to contain everyone in the wedding party in one area so that no one got lost or decided to explore the territory.

The terminal staff would usually direct wedding guests to the check-in area. That's when I'd meet the couple, who'd be given complete instructions and told that there'd always be someone by their side to ensure they were given the best service they could've bought.

There were two types of check-in procedures. One was for "non-sailing guests" who would not be staying on board the cruise. They were usually only there to see the ceremony, stay for the reception, and then disembark the ship when an announcement was made to do so.

Then we had the sailing guests, which of course, included the bride and groom, members of the bridal party, and often most family members. These sailing guests would be taken to the computer area to check in with the documentation they'd received from the ship to receive their "sea cards." These cards would get them into their cabin as well as act as charge cards that would allow them to make purchases for the duration of the cruise.

Security would be very important prior to boarding the ship. Every guest that didn't sail would be required to provide the couple with the form of identification they planned to use to obtain a "visitors' pass" prior to boarding. This form of ID could be a driver's license, passport, or any other form of photo ID that would be acceptable to the ship.

WEDDING CHRONICLES

The necessary information would be provided to the couple in advance so that they could pass the information on to their guests. Without the proper ID, guests would not be permitted to board. This applies to children and even infants. There really were no exceptions to the rule!

A boarding manifest would be used at the check-in area. The person boarding would then leave their ID with a staff member to receive their visitors' pass, allowing them to board the ship when it was time. After the event was over and they began leaving the ship, they'd return to the same check-in area, return the visitors' passes, and collect their IDs.

Once every one of the guests received their visitors' pass, they'd be brought to a comfortable seating area. After all the sailing guests arrived (and they were usually the first to arrive), they'd be intermingled with the non-sailing guests. Lots of hugs and kisses were sure to be exchanged at this point.

When we were given the OK to go through security, we'd bring all the guests in to go through X-ray machines for a stringent security check.

The non-sailing guests would be escorted to a special seating section designated for the "wedding party" with a sign that indicates this. The sailing guests would be escorted to the computer section to receive their boarding papers and cabin keys, among other things.

When all the check-in procedures have been met, it'll become a waiting game for customs and immigration to give the word that the ship is ready for boarding. We must wait for every passenger on the ship from the prior cruise to leave before anyone else can board.

One of the perks that wedding couples get is priority boarding, which means that the wedding party and their guests board the ship before regular passengers. This allows the couple to get to their cabin without fighting past the crowd and for their guests to more easily be escorted to the ceremony location to await the ceremony.

"Just to give you some idea as to the time frame that we have to work with," Maria said, "it flows like this. The full wedding party and guests will arrive by 10 a.m. We'll get them checked in and get the visitors' passes for those that aren't sailing. We'll all go through security, and then we'll need to get the sailing guests their necessary boarding papers and cabin keys by about 10:45 a.m.

"After all the boarding procedures are accomplished, we'll wait in the final waiting area. With a little luck, the ship coordinator will come down to greet us and tell us that we'll probably board the ship at about 11 a.m. or 11:30 a.m.

"About 5-10 minutes prior to boarding the ship, I'll make a pre-boarding announcement advising all those attending the event exactly where and when the wedding will take place, and some boarding as well as disembarking procedures so they'll know what to expect. When we board, we'll board as one large group. The coordinators will take their positions to see that everyone is grouped while they're escorted to the ship."

If we boarded a little early, guests would tend to visit different areas of the ship out of curiosity, but they'd be told they must return to the ceremony location at least 15 minutes before the start of the ceremony. Otherwise, the doors might be closed, and they'd miss the ceremony.

"No one has ever missed the ceremony," Maria mused, "except those guests that arrived very late at the terminal. But they're still able to board to at least be at the reception. We always leave word at the check-in desk at the times when the ceremony and reception are being held just for latecomers who can't get to the ship when they're supposed to. That does happen quite a bit."

Once we boarded, the bridal couple would be escorted by the lead coordinator to their cabin to get dressed. Perhaps another cabin or two would also be made available for members of the wedding party.

Cabins would initially only be available for the couple and their wedding party. Other sailing couples would need to wait until it was announced by the ship that they were ready for all passengers, including other regular cruisers.

"The ceremony, in most cases, will start at about 12:15 or 12:30," Maria added. "They will finish in about 20-30 minutes, and immediately after, the reception will begin."

Music would be played throughout the event, including ceremony music and any variety of songs that the couple could choose from if they so wished. They could also just leave it to the lead coordinator to recommend the selection of music to be used.

After Maria had given me my fill of all these little details, I realized it was almost showtime. The ceremony was about to begin!

When I'd first met the couple upon their arrival at the terminal, I'd given them some idea of what to expect during the ceremony and the boarding procedure, so they'd had somewhat of a brief rehearsal.

It was given to them again by the lead coordinator moments before the bridal party entered, and the bride was thus ready to enter when the ceremony began.

As the music played, "Ladies and gentlemen, will you please rise for the bride?" rang out over the crowd of guests.

I have a few little tricks, in general, that play very well when I perform a ceremony. I'll often tell the bride to stop about 25 feet from where the groom is standing. Then I'll tell the groom, "go get your bride!" Naturally, I'll use their names. It always brings out the "oohs and ahhs" from their guests.

Once the couple stands before me, my ceremony takes about 20 minutes. Immediately following the ceremony, the couple is shuffled off to a quiet area where the photographer takes some photos. In the meantime, the room is prepared for dancing and the reception. This all occurs once the bridal party is announced, with the wedding couple to follow.

The couple can make arrangements when booking a wedding as to the food they'd like to have served, and there are always many different choices. From passed hors d'oeuvres to buffet-style food of all kinds to a beautiful sit-down luncheon with fine wine and impeccable service, the sky's the limit, and some ships are truly magnificent when it comes to their cuisine and service. You have to see it to believe it, and I've certainly seen it.

Before I knew it, the party was almost over. The bride and groom had their first dance; a dad had danced with his daughter, and a mom with her son, and everyone was happy. It was time to say goodbye.

The ship coordinators (sometimes called GSCs for Group Service Coordinators) helped quite a bit during the wedding.

They'd had the wherewithal and all the information in hand to get things done if we needed them to. They could make the room cooler by calling the engineer, bringing in more tables for wedding favors, and requesting more food if there wasn't enough. In short, they'd helped us to make everything perfect for the couple.

At about 2:15 or 2:30 (and sometimes it might even go to 3:00 if the ship got in a few minutes late or changed departure time), I was informed that either I or the lead coordinator would make the announcement for all non-sailing guests to prepare to leave with some added instructions on how to disembark. Many were usually escorted off by a coordinator, and some just naturally wandered off by themselves.

Our team was the last group to leave the ship to ensure that the couple had such a wonderful time that they'd remember it for the rest of their lives. Couples usually recognized the great service they were provided with and generally would give all those that helped facilitate their wedding with great service a fair gratuity.

Wedding number one was finished, and everyone was happy, so I asked Maria when the next wedding would be.

"Next Saturday," she said simply.

"You're kidding!" I replied. "You're going back tonight! What do I do for my team?"

"Well, Jennifer and Rachel will be here if you like, and you can make the arrangements to hire some more coordinators until you get the feel for how many you'll need. I'll have Buck call you to give you some more information as to what team members are paid and some thoughts as to how you can recruit them."

"Well, I guess that'll do for now, and I have a few ideas of my own that I think will help. But please tell Buck to call me as soon as possible."

I asked Jennifer and Rachel to work on these weddings with me until I could get some more girls to join us. They agreed, and that took some of the pressure off me for the time being.

Next Saturday would come quickly enough, so I had to start finding some people to coordinate these weddings. I knew it would take a little work.

I didn't have enough time to place an ad, so I thought I would try to recruit some girls by stopping them and asking if they wanted to be wedding coordinators. I know it sounds kind of ridiculous, but the fact of the matter is that it worked.

For example, the very next time I used a Dunkin' Donuts drive-through for coffee, I asked the girl that handed it to me, "would you like to be a wedding coordinator on a cruise ship?"

"I'd love to!" she exclaimed.

I handed her my card and told her to call me. She did that evening.

CAPTAIN ARNOLD WONSEVER

When I drove by a bus stop and saw a few girls waiting for a bus, I rolled down my window and shouted, "Any of you girls want a job as a wedding coordinator on a cruise ship?" I handed out a few cards, and some called.

If I stopped to have lunch at a diner or went to a restaurant in the evening with my wife to have dinner, I handed out my business cards to some of the waitresses. "If you'd like to give some thought about being a wedding coordinator on a beautiful cruise ship, call me!" I said. "It's mostly on weekends and only about 5 hours of easy, fun-filled work." Again, some called, and some took me up on the offer.

I did the same thing wherever I saw bodies that could help do the job, at least until I was able to place an ad and hire a team that I could train to be professional coordinators. I simply did what I had to in order to create a small team to work with me until I had the time to really put the team together that would work for me in the years ahead.

In the beginning, it was important to have some coordinators that had a nice appearance and followed instructions so that the couple and their guests felt that they were in the hands of professionals.

As the months went on and a few years had passed, I found enough wedding coordinators to satisfy the number of weddings that were given to me, but the writing was on the wall that I had to prepare for a much larger number of weddings that were coming my way.

Because more and more weddings were being given to me on different ships, it was time to increase the size of my team, and I felt it was time to place a nice ad in the *New York Times*.

Instead, a neighbor who'd worked for our local town newspaper suggested that I place the ad on Craig's List, which at the time was not as widely known as it is now.

"'Craig's List?' What's that?" I asked.

"Just go to 'Craigslist.com,' and you'll find out," she said.

Boy, was she right about that!

I wrote a beautiful ad saying, "Wedding Coordinators Needed for Major Cruise Ships - Part-Time Only." The copy was as strong as the headline.

I made a mistake, however, of listing my cell phone number for candidates to call. My phone wouldn't stop ringing, so I immediately removed the number and had everyone reply by sending me a cover letter with some reasons why they'd like to be wedding coordinators, along with a resume.

I received over 100 replies on the first day and about half that on the second day. I had to remove the listing by the end of the second day. At this point, I felt I had enough replies to build my team (or what I like to call my "navy") of truly great wedding coordinators.

Now I was finally able to speak to each one that replied to the listing and hired those that I felt would be right for the job. That solved my problem with finding the right people.

Some of these coordinators have now been with me for years - several for almost 10 years and a few for about 8 years. These are my team leaders, and I consider them to be the best of the best in the service they provide to my wedding couples and their guests.

I also needed to hire several ministers, photographers, videographers, and DJs. I'd started receiving requests from couples who asked to have these vendors for their weddings when ships could not supply them, so it was necessary for me to create a full team of wedding service providers. This didn't last but a few years because the ships themselves began to provide many of these wedding services to maintain an additional source of income.

So here we are in 2018, and almost 13 years have passed. I'm still performing wedding ceremonies on many different cruise ships and orchestrating and running the entire operation from beginning to end. I have about 20-25 wedding coordinators that work on these weddings, and I try to keep that number to meet the requirements dictated to me by the ships where the weddings will take place. My current team helps me to service these weddings in the most professional way possible.

The cruise ships that promote these weddings want the bridal couple and their guests to feel secure in the knowledge that when the couple decided to get married on their ship, they were guaranteed to have a wedding in an atmosphere full of love and beauty, with memories that the couple will remember for the rest of their lives. And that's what I do: create beautiful memories.

The future looks even brighter from what I see.

If you're curious, here's a listing of all the ships where I've helped to create these beautiful memories for many hundreds of couples:

Norwegian Cruise Lines:

The Gem, Dawn, Spirit, Sun, Crown, Jewel, Star, Pearl, and the Breakaway

Royal Caribbean Cruise Lines:

The Voyager of the Seas, Explorer of the Seas, and Anthem of the Seas.

Celebrity Cruise Lines:

The Zenith and the Summit

Princess Cruise Lines:

The Crown Princess and Caribbean Princess

Queen Mary II and **Disney Magic Cruise Ship**

CAPTAIN ARNOLD WONSEVER

It Was Heard Around the World

George and Smita had their wedding at a beautiful hillside overlooking the Hudson River Valley in South Salem, New York. It was called "Le Chateau" and was built by J.P. Morgan as a gift for his friend and former minister (what a gift!).

I arrived early, as usual, to check out the grounds and see that everything was in place for the ceremony. I noticed an array of sophisticated computer equipment a few feet from where the ceremony was to take place.

I asked George about it, thinking that maybe they would take some "home movies."

"Captain," he replied, "your ceremony will be seen and heard worldwide at the same time you will be performing it - in India, the UK, Belgium and the Czech Republic.

"That's where Smita and I have family and friends who could not be here today, and you know the old saying: 'If Mohammad can't come to the mountain, then let's bring the mountain to Mohammad'."

It seems they made arrangements with their friend Abby, who was, without question, a "computer genius" and would oversee setting up this broadcast.

A few weeks after the wedding, I received an email from

WEDDING CHRONICLES

George and Smita telling me that the broadcast to their family and friends was a great success. They had all seen and heard the ceremony as it was being performed, and the different time zones hadn't mattered at all. Ah, the wonderful world of computer technology and the internet. Where in the world would we be without it?

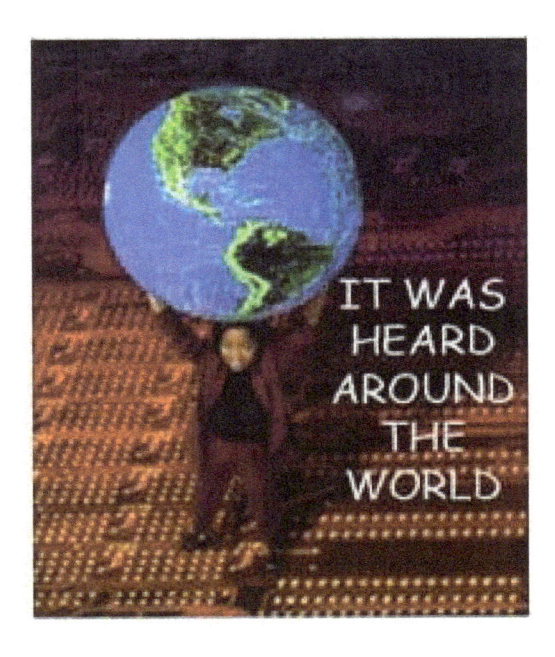

CAPTAIN ARNOLD WONSEVER

It Just Had To Be on the Queen Mary II

I love this little story, and I think you will too. Tess and Jay contacted me early in May and told me that they would like to get married on the Queen Mary II, a cruise ship that today is considered one of the world's greatest cruise ships afloat.

Tess's mom was 88 years old and currently in good health. Not knowing how long she would stay that way, they decided to treat her to a cruise on the QM-2 while the ship would be in New York harbor over the July 4th weekend.

Tess and Jay had been engaged for about a year but had to postpone their wedding several times due to her mom's ill health. Now, things looked promising, and, as Tess put it, hopefully they could get their license and set things in motion to make this very special day of theirs happen now on the QM-2.

There was only one problem that seemed to hinder their plans. I already had three weddings scheduled to perform that day, and this would be the fourth. My concern was if there would be enough time to allow me to do it. But Lady Luck was with them, and I guess she was with me too. I was available.

Before long, however, more problems arose. Tess and Jay had contacted Cunard Lines to get permission for me to come aboard the ship to perform the ceremony, but due to very tight security after

9/11, especially on cruise ships such as the QM-2, they had persistently refused Tess and Jay's requests.

A change of plans was then put into motion. They decided to get married on July 1st at the "Water Club" in Manhattan, or the "River Café" in Brooklyn, followed by a dinner celebration.

I could tell from talking to Tess and by some of her emails to me that she and Jay still had their hearts set on getting married on the QM-2, with her mom present, in what could only be called a "fairy tale" event. It was enough for them to rekindle their search for a way, or a loophole, to get me on the ship to perform the ceremony.

Tess then emailed me and asked if I would contact the ship directly. Perhaps, as one Captain to another, and with all my credentials, I could convince the ship's Captain to let me perform the ceremony.

Days passed quickly, and we really had to move, so I was about to start making some inquiries of my own to find a person who had the authority to allow an exception to the rule.

Before I reached anyone, I heard from Tess about her new idea.

"I looked everywhere last night," she said, "on their boarding papers and on their website. Everywhere it emphatically states that non-paying guests are not allowed on the ship for security reasons. This was when I came up with a wonderful idea…let's make you a *paid* passenger!!"

And on that note, they bought me a passenger ticket. With that ticket, I would be able to board the ship, perform their ceremony, and even take the cruise if I so desired. When I asked Tess what I should do with the ticket otherwise, she said to keep it as a memento.

And so, the wheels were in motion for me to be able to board the QM-2 to perform their ceremony. I would be given the QM-2 special ID card giving me an "open gangway" to move about the ship with no restrictions.

I met with Tess and Jay a few weeks before the wedding day and received the very impressive leather pouch embossed with the QM-2 insignia, my passenger ticket enclosed.

Their wedding day came, and we planned to meet at about 2:00 pm in the Commodore Club on their stateroom deck. When I arrived at the ship around 12:45 pm, I was astonished to see what looked like thousands of people waiting in a very long line to board the ship.

"Hmm… I'm a Captain," I thought to myself, "so why not do what Captains do?"

WEDDING CHRONICLES

I walked right to the front of the line, showed the security and crew my ID card, and they even acknowledged me with a snappy salute and a "welcome aboard, Captain."

I got into an elevator, went up to Deck 9, and waited in the Club. See their note to me for the rest of the story, especially the postscript.

I would have loved to have gone on that cruise on one of the world's greatest cruise ships, but duty called, and I still had two more couples waiting for me, looking forward to their own fairy-tale weddings.

Bon voyage Tess, Jay, and Mom. I'll sure remember this one!!!

CAPTAIN ARNOLD WONSEVER

Dear Captain Arnold:

We just got off the QM2 and immediately wanted to write and thank you for making our much-anticipated wedding day so wonderful. We thought a spectacular ship like Queen Mary II would be romantic and special, but you made it even more so. Your room selection, complete with a fireplace, had wonderful intimacy. Your words were heartfelt, and our vows made everyone misty-eyed. Thank you for paying special attention to my mom, who kept saying you were wonderful.

And thank you so much for arranging for our cabin steward, Karen, to take our pictures after the ceremony. You can tell how blissful we were on our wedding day, with each picture better than the next.

Warmest Regards,

Tess and Jay

By the way, the ship called Mom before disembarkation looking for you. We told them you had an emergency and could not return for the voyage!

They Found Love at a Citgo Gas Station

At about 11: 00 in the morning, on a hot August day, I received a phone call from a young lady. "Sir, can you perform a marriage?" she very hurriedly and nervously asked. Then, almost afraid to say it, she added, "Today?"

Even though I already had one wedding ceremony to perform that day, I politely replied that I could.

She further explained that I had been recommended to her by a client of mine who was a yacht broker. When I heard "yacht broker," I immediately thought she and her fiancée had planned a wedding on a yacht and needed my services.

But then I thought to myself that if they were getting married on a yacht or even on one of the many "dinner cruise" ships that go around Manhattan, there had to have been a lot of planning involved. Surely, they would have retained the services of a wedding officiant long *before* the day of the ceremony. At this point, I was very intrigued and wanted to hear more.

She went on to explain that their marriage license was from New Jersey, and she had had a little "accident" with it. It might be torn a little.

She meant to say that she and her fiancée had had an

argument, and she had been so mad at him that she had begun to tear up the license.

I told her that they had to have a brand new, intact license if they wanted to get married that day. The State of New Jersey would not accept a license with an error, crossed-out words, or even whiteout on it. I suggested that she call the license bureau and find out if they needed a new one and, if so, if they could obtain it that day.

She then asked if I would be able to come that day to where they were in New Jersey. I asked where they were.

"In a gas station," she replied.

I could hardly believe my ears, and I asked her again where they were asking me to marry them.

"Yes," she said, repeating, "at a Citgo gas station."

For a moment, I thought one of my friends was playing a joke on me. I really didn't think I was hearing correctly.

"I'm performing a ceremony at 3:30 in Central Park for a couple from Scotland," I said to her. "After you get the new, clean, unblemished marriage license and everything is in order, call me back at around 4:00 pm and let's see if you still want me to come out to where you are."

At 4:05, my cell phone rang; this time, it was the groom on the other end. He almost impatiently asked, "So, what time do you think you'll be here?"

"Where?" I asked.

"Here at my gas station in New Jersey. We want to get married, and we want you to perform our ceremony, so here are the directions. When you get over the George Washington Bridge, take 80 West to exit 64B. Make a left at the light and stop at the first Citgo Gas Station. That's where we'll be."

"Hmmm," I thought to myself, "no deposit, no emails, no consultations, nothing in writing, just a phone call from two people that really don't sound too convincing."

But what the heck? It was only a 45-minute drive from where I was, and the weather was warm but beautiful. It was a nice day for a drive, and I would find out if this was for real.

Thus, I began my journey into the "twilight zone." As I left Central Park and began my drive through Manhattan to New Jersey, my curiosity about this couple grew. I couldn't decide if they were some exotic, bizarre couple or just a couple in love, willing to do anything to get married as quickly as possible.

When I arrived at the gas station, I asked the first person I saw about the ceremony. I think he was a mechanic.

"So," I said, "who's getting married?"

He looked at me rather strangely, as if wondering who would

get married at a gas station, but then he asked someone else there a few questions in another language. He soon directed me to a small office, and that was where I saw Mary for the first time.

She was sitting on the floor with her back against the wall. Her arms were wrapped around her knees, which were pulled up to her chin. She was looking at me with eyes that were sad but filled with warmth and a certain beauty that only a bride radiates.

"Is it you that's getting married?" I inquired.

She replied by nodding her head.

"And where is the groom, your fiancé?" I asked.

At that, she pointed to Izmir, who was standing by a gas pump saying goodbye to a customer. I then asked where they would like me to perform the ceremony, and she pointed to the garage next to the office.

She asked me if she could wear the veil and get the flowers she had bought for the occasion.

I told her that, of course, she should wear her veil and get her flowers. What kind of bride would she be without a veil and flowers?

On that note, she ran out of the office to an SUV that was parked outside. She prettied herself up with some lipstick and a little makeup, brushed her hair, and placed the veil on her head. She was beginning to look like a real bride.

Wanting to create a softer, more romantic atmosphere, she had brought a candle to light during the ceremony. Her flowers were artificial, but her love and passion were as real as could be.

"C'mon, it's time," she called out to Izmir. "You can't keep the Captain waiting. Pull down the garage door, and let's get started."

There was no champagne to make a toast, guests, reception, food, or music. There was just the heavy odor of grease, oil, and gas on a hot, humid day in August.

Then I thought about that candle she wanted to light. With the smell of gas all around us, it might be the last ceremony I'd perform if she lit that candle, so I told her to hold off until after the ceremony was finished, and we opened the garage door.

The air was so thick that you could cut it with a knife. The only people there were Mary and Izmir, me, their mechanic as a witness, and one passerby from Florida who had stopped to buy some gas. He was asked to be a witness too.

As I stood there watching Mary get ready for her wedding, I thought about how this was still probably the most important day of her life. While it was a far cry from what weddings were usually like, at that moment in time, they seemed to be the happiest couple in the world.

She told me they had gotten their license just the day before and did not want to wait to marry. They were perfectly happy having their ceremony at the Citgo gas station on the highway in New Jersey - she with her pretty little veil, wearing white shorts and a white tank top, and Izmir in his gas station work shirt with the Citgo logo on it.

So, there we were at the gas station, next to a grease pit, automotive parts, and used flat tires and hub caps, with tools all over the place and a broken down, old car in the garage that they must have taken apart for parts.

"Do you have the rings?" I asked.

"Rings...?" they echoed.

Uh oh! I guess we needed some rings.

Luckily, I found some old, rusted washers (I took them off some nuts and bolts), and those became their wedding rings, at least for the moment. After all, it was just for symbolic purposes. I told them that later that they could buy real rings and throw away the washers, but who would throw away the washers they got married in??

Mary cried as they said their vows, and tears began rolling down her cheeks. Izmir smiled and held her face in his hands, wiping away the tears. After the ceremony, Mary and Izmir kissed like all couples do when they hear, "I now pronounce you husband and wife."

Within minutes after finishing the ceremony and kissing his

bride, Izmir left to pump gas into the next car that pulled up.

Then I left them there - two people in love. As he watched the gas pump meter ticking away at $2.53 a gallon, she stood at the cash register waiting for the money. She removed her veil and wiped away some of her tears. She wanted to give me the flowers she had carried, but I said no. She asked me if I needed some gas, but again, I said no. I had filled it up earlier.

As I pulled out of the station on my way back to New York, I thought to myself that this one was really a gas and definitely one for the books. But you know what? I felt good about this one. Even as I was sitting in bumper-to-bumper traffic at the George Washington Bridge on my way home, I know one thing's for sure: the next time I pull into a Citgo gas station and say, "Fill'er up!" I'll always think of Mary and Izmir.

Up, Up and Away!

"Would you be our 'flying wedding officiant' and help us realize our dream?" Adam and Bonnie asked me in an email in March of 2005.

"This should be interesting," I thought to myself, "but perhaps before I say yes, I should check my insurance and make sure that my parachute is in good working order!"

Adam and Bonnie, a lovely Austrian couple living in Vienna, were planning to come to America. They would get married in a helicopter high above New York City, spend a little time in New York, and then journey home on the Queen Mary II. Now that's what I call getting married with the special ingredients of thrills and luxury!

I replied to Adam that I would be happy to be their "flying wedding officiant," and the wheels were set in motion for the wedding to take place on October 14th, 2005. It was a very significant date as it was both Bonnie's and my birthday. A wedding and two birthdays…what a day that was going to be!

Months passed, and we kept in touch via email. Adam advised me from time to time on the status of the arrangements he had made with Liberty Helicopter, the largest helicopter sightseeing and charter service in the Northeast.

More months flew by, and on October 11th, Adam and Bonnie arrived in a very wet and soggy New York. One may recall that it rained for eight days during that time and that people living in some New Jersey towns were getting around the streets in little boats.

Adam called me then, and we set up a meeting the next day at the New Yorker Hotel in New York City. The rain was relentless and didn't let up for a moment. I met with the couple for the first time over a light lunch and chatted a bit about the wedding.

We also spent a few minutes talking to a reporter from the *New York Post* who'd gotten wind of Adam and Bonnie's story and their plans of getting married in a helicopter. It must have been newsworthy. After all, how many people got married in a helicopter?

I also learned that Adam was an IT consultant and Bonnie was a gynecologist. As an IT consultant, Adam was somewhat of a genius when it came to computers and his networking capabilities. This later proved to be a tremendous help to me.

During lunch, I briefly mentioned to Adam that I was having a few problems with my computer system and could not network my laptop and desktop computer together. In a second, Adam and Bonnie offered to come to my home and fix my problem. "Whew!"

I thought to myself. "This really is a special couple!"

The rain and the flooding did not let up, and the inconveniences that this caused were too numerous to mention. I remember Adam emailing me one day, saying he had a bad dream. What would happen if the bad weather prevented the helicopter from flying?

Well, it seemed like his dream came true for that Friday, October 14th. Adam received a call from the helicopter company and was advised that the date had been moved up to Saturday the 15th due to the negative forecast.

But when Saturday came, it was beautiful. It was a warm, sunny day that was perfect for flying, with a sky clear enough for you to see forever.

I met Adam and Bonnie at the Downtown Heliport at about noon. The people in the Heliport were smiling and wishing them luck, and some even applauded when they realized that Adam and Bonnie were a bride and groom going up in a helicopter to be married.

We were given some last-minute instructions pertaining to safety and looked at a quick video before boarding. Next thing we knew, we were in the helicopter. We met the pilot Jack, and Adam, Bonnie, and I were given headsets with microphones to communicate.

Barney, our photographer, had flown in from Vienna the day before. He sat in the front seat next to the pilot, and I sat in the back with Adam and Bonnie.

In a few moments, the roar of the engines told us we were on our way. The street, the buildings, the people, and the cars all got smaller. The voice coming out of our headsets was the pilot talking to air traffic control.

When our altitude was about 1,500 feet or so, I began my ceremony. The cockpit is quickly filled with an atmosphere of love and happiness that only a bride and groom can radiate. It took about 17 minutes, and during that time, I could also hear voices through my headset, which led me to believe other people were listening in on that channel and probably heard my ceremony as well.

The flight was amazing and lasted about 45 minutes over New York City and beyond. We took a few turns here and there so that we could see the Statue of Liberty, the Verrazano Bridge, and the Yankee Stadium. We could almost reach out and shake hands with people on top of the Empire State Building. For Adam and Bonnie, it really was their special day.

The ceremony was soon over, and I pronounced them husband and wife. We heard so many voices come over the headsets that were being worn saying "congratulations", and it sounded like it was all coming from out of the clouds.

CAPTAIN ARNOLD WONSEVER

That following Tuesday, Adam and Bonnie visited my home, and Adam fixed my computer problems. They met my wife, and we all went to a lovely Italian restaurant for a great dinner. They boarded the Queen Mary II for their honeymoon journey back home on Thursday.

They stopped in London for a day and then went back to Vienna, where, on October 29th, they had a very large reception and shared their New York experience with their friends and loved ones. When I finally asked Adam and Bonnie why they had wanted to get married in a helicopter, they simply replied, "We just wanted to get away from the crowd."

Adam and Bonnie, my friends across the sea, thank you for having let me come into your lives to play such an important role on your wedding day. It was a unique and unusual wedding ceremony, and I will remember it for many years.

WEDDING CHRONICLES

Till Death Do Us Part

It was 8 am on December 16th, 2005, when the phone rang. My wife answered it.

"Can I speak with the Captain?" the voice on the other end asked.

She handed me the phone, and a somewhat distressed, saddened man's voice said to me, "My name is Mario. Can you marry us today?"

"Where? And why so quickly?" I asked.

"My wife is very, very sick," he replied. "We were married once but had gotten divorced. She has cancer now and is dying, so we want to remarry."

My mind went blank for a moment, and I was at a loss for words. What comforting words can one offer at a time like this?

"How long does she have?" I asked.

"Twelve hours, two days...maybe one month," he said. "They told me that ten days ago at the hospital, but she's still with us. She's a fighter.

"The hospital just released her yesterday," Mario went on to say. "They said there was nothing else they could do for her. I drove with her then to the marriage license bureau in New York City. She waited in the car, and the chief of staff came down to see her. Due to the circumstances and her terminal illness, they issued us the marriage license right away."

"Where do you want me to perform the ceremony? I asked.

"In my home," he replied. "Only our son and daughter will be there."

Mario also told me that he had been advised by the person he'd met at the license bureau that they would issue him their marriage certificate immediately if he brought the completed marriage license back after the wedding ceremony.

I called the bureau to verify this because, under normal circumstances, the officiant must return the license within five days after the ceremony and the marriage certificate is usually mailed to the couple four to six weeks later. Given the circumstance involved, they could make exceptions to the rule. I cleared my schedule, and the wedding ceremony was scheduled for 4 pm.

As the hours passed, I couldn't help but think about how I would structure my ceremony to fit the situation that would soon be before me. Of all the wedding ceremonies I'd performed, this was the first time I felt I was performing a wedding ceremony and a funeral service at the same time. It was a bizarre feeling if ever there was one.

At 3:45 pm, I arrived at their home. Mario was waiting on the front porch to greet me. He walked me around to the back of the house and motioned me to come up the stairs that led to the kitchen entrance. We waited at the kitchen entrance and spoke for a while.

It was then that he shook my hand and thanked me for coming. I embraced him and couldn't find the words I wanted to say to him. I could only imagine what he must be going through at this time.

But then my comforting words began to flow as we stood there, and Mario told me about their life together and why they wanted to remarry after 27 years of divorce. While he spoke, his eyes began to fill up with tears.

His children were inside the house. He didn't want them to see him crying, so he wiped away his tears, saying, "I have to be strong for the kids."

The kitchen door opened just then. His son, Mario Jr., was standing there with his sister Christy. With his outstretched hand, Mario Jr. shook my hand firmly and said, "Thank you for coming, sir." Christy approached me and hugged me.

As soon as I walked in, I knew that sickness and death were close by. I could smell the medication and the aroma that you could easily detect in a hospital. As I was led into the living room adjacent to the dining room (where the ceremony would take place), I could see that the entire area had apparently been converted into a large bedroom.

I could also see the enormous amounts of medication sitting on the dining room table and all the medical equipment that was attached to the person lying in bed there. It was then that I first saw Debby lying in a hospital bed that was obviously brought into the room to make her comfortable.

When she saw me, she smiled and held out her hand to greet me. In a faint voice, she said, "Thank you for coming."

Even in sickness, she was a pretty lady, but it was easy to see that her terminal illness had drained the color from her face, and her pain medication had made her somewhat incoherent. She waved me closer and whispered, "My only regret, Captain, is that I won't be able to go on my honeymoon."

I choked up on those words and immediately changed the mood by smiling at her and telling her what beautiful children she had. Her daughter went to reach for the camera to take a few pictures only to find out the batteries were dead, so I reached into my bag, removed my Sony camera, and handed it to her.

"Take as many pictures as you like," I said. After all, what would a wedding be without photographs?

"Is there anything you need, Captain?" Mario asked, and he

told his son to fetch me a cold drink in the same breath. I was getting ready to perform the ceremony, and I told Mario to take a chair and sit next to Debby rather than stand beside her alongside the bed. This would bring them closer together.

Their children were serving as witnesses and had also signed the license. They, too, were standing beside them.

My ceremony began, but it wasn't the usual ceremony. My words were changed in so many places to fit the situation. As I performed the ceremony, I looked at their faces and saw happiness and sadness at the same time. Death was knocking at their door, but they were facing it, smiling.

It was really hard for me, and as much as I tried not to show it, my voice reflected the emotional and moving feeling that I experienced during those precious words of endearment. When I asked them to repeat their vows, they cried, and so did their children.

I never used some of the words you'd find in many standard vows, like "in sickness and in health" or "till death do you part." This was certainly not the time for those words, and, in keeping with my usual self, I injected some words of humor to bring some smiles and just a little laughter into this home. It was welcomed by all, especially Debby.

In a little while, the ceremony was over. Debby kissed me then, and Mario held my hand and thanked me profusely. The children did likewise. As Mario walked me out of the house to my car, he told me he would be in touch and keep me posted.

I got into my car and drove away, saying to myself, "I hope I never have to do a ceremony like this again!"

 "Debby died on January 18th, 2006, but she lives on in the minds of her family."

An Accident That Saved Her Life

While I was in Florida enjoying my usual annual vacation, I received a call from Joyce. She told me she was planning a wedding reception for her daughter Barbara on Saturday, June 24, 2006.

She told me that she wanted to hold the wedding reception at her home in Roslyn Heights, New York and that she would handle all the arrangements for her daughter and her fiancé. She further advised me that all communications and acknowledgment should be done directly with her.

The months flew by very quickly, and approximately four weeks before the wedding, I sent out my usual bride and groom checklist so that I would have the information I needed to prepare for the ceremony.

A few days before the day of the ceremony, I received a call from Joyce.

"Captain," she said, "I have some bad news for you."

"Here's another wedding that bites the dust," I immediately thought to myself. "The bride and groom will each go their own merry way." But I was never more wrong.

"What happened?" I asked.

"Barbara is in intensive care in the hospital," Joyce replied. "She had a brain tumor removed two days ago." Strangely enough, her next question was: "Could they still get their marriage license without her being there?"

I indicated that it was possible, and, in some cases, the marriage license bureau would send a representative to the hospital to assist in issuing the license if medical circumstances warranted it. I told her that I would make some phone calls to inquire if this could be arranged since the marriage was still going to take place. It might not be on the original date, but it would be close.

I proceeded to make my calls. I found out that the medical note indicated that the severity of the condition would, in fact, apply and that the marriage license bureau would make arrangements with a representative. This representative would visit the location and attest to the fact that the license could be issued given the extenuating circumstances.

I thought about it for a while and then said to Joyce, "Why is a wedding in such a situation? Why not wait until she feels better and returns to her old self again? Then, you could have the wedding in a happier atmosphere. She could always get her license with Mitchell when she is feeling better and can drive to the license bureau."

They took my advice.

Days passed, and on July 4, I heard from Barbara.

"It's wonderful to hear your voice," I said. "Your mom told me about the hospital. I'll make myself available when you need me, but the most important thing right now is for you to get well and put this situation behind you. What happened?"

She told me her story then, which was truly amazing.

While she was at work, she had received an electric shock. Apparently, she had touched some electrical cord that caused the shock.

"I was almost electrocuted, and it really hurt," she said. "My arm started to hurt me very badly. I went to my doctor, and during his examination, he said he wanted to take a CAT scan just to play it safe.

"While my arms were hurting, I was also getting bad headaches. That was when the CAT scan revealed a tumor on my brain. I was told it'd been there since I was a little girl, but the shock I received moved it. Had it not been discovered by the CAT scan, it would've only been a matter of time before it would've been inoperable, and I'd be gone. They scheduled immediate surgery to remove it.

"It all happened so fast that I just couldn't believe it. So, in a sense, this accident also saved my life."

On that note, she asked if I was available to perform her

ceremony on Thursday, July 6, at her apartment in New York. It would make her feel more comfortable than the car drive to her mom's home in Long Island.

"Sure," I replied. "Let's do it."

Many guests attended and, needless to say, they all knew what happened to Barbara. Tears of happiness were flowing from just about everyone but, most of all, from Joyce, Barbara's mom. It was a beautiful rooftop wedding in Manhattan, and the view was spectacular.

But the most important thing of all was that these two wonderful people, Barbara and Mitchell, were able to have their wedding day, and I was happy to be there to perform their ceremony. It had been a somewhat tragic beginning, but it had ended on a happy note.

WEDDING CHRONICLES

A Million-Dollar Wedding

Another wedding ceremony that I performed was at a beautiful venue called the "Lighthouse" on July 2, 2005. It was located at Chelsea Piers, a waterfront area in New York City that's well-known as the home of the many large and luxurious motor yachts belonging to the rich and the famous.

A few popular dinner cruise boats also make Chelsea Piers their home port and cater to the general public. Their clientele often includes local New York residents and many travelers, especially those coming from out of town to see New York City's famous sites and landmarks from a different view beyond what they'd get from a sightseeing bus.

The Lighthouse is what I'd consider an upscale wedding venue (and an easy sell) because of the magnificent view from its property. It hugs the water as New York Harbor is adjacent to it, and the New Jersey shoreline is only a couple hundred yards across from it.

Major cruise ships sail by it constantly throughout the day when they're leaving this body of water for the open sea. The view during the day or night is so beautiful that some would say it's breathtaking. I've performed several wedding ceremonies at this location, and I can also vouch for their excellent cuisine and service, both of which are way above the norm.

I'm telling you all this because, while the Lighthouse may

be where this particular wedding story technically began, almost 2 years later, almost to the day, it ends up somewhere else. I know this might sound a little confusing, and I'm sure that when my editor reads this, he'll laugh and think to himself, "Boy, how can I move his words around so that this will make sense?!"

As I may have indicated in previous stories, I like to arrive at the wedding venue about 45 minutes to an hour earlier than the scheduled ceremony. This way, I have all the time I need to meet with the couple and review all of the important things related to the ceremony, especially in cases where the photographers seem to take over and forget that there's even a ceremony.

Firstly, it's crucial that I take care of their wedding license and have it signed by the couple's witnesses. Then there are things that need to be done, such as checking the ceremony location to ensure everything's in order.

I also like to have some words with the bridal attendant or the maître d' in charge of sending down the processional. This is because I have my own unique way of presenting the groom to the bride at the start of a ceremony. When I tell the bride to stop and instruct the groom to "go get your bride," it never fails to bring out a few "oohs" and "ahhs" from a crowd!

The couple whose ceremony I initially performed this time, Bernard and Laura, were just wonderful from the day we first spoke until after the ceremony. When it was time for me to leave, they insisted that I join their guests and stay for dinner. I politely declined but offered to stay for at least the cocktail hour. "Absolutely!" was their emphatic response.

While their wonderful wedding is still not the one I mean to discuss, it's funny how fate works. Sometimes, being in the right place at the right time causes things to happen. I guess some things were just meant to be, and that is how my real story begins.

As you know, at every wedding there is music. All kinds of music - from steel drums, accordions, and harmonicas, to DJs, small bands, string quartets, and sometimes even a large orchestra.

I felt that the music at this wedding was very special from the moment I heard the group play. Their "getting ready" music, seating music, ceremony music, and even their "warming up" music were some of the best I'd ever heard. It caught my attention immediately, and even more so since the source of this greatness was hidden behind a curtain a little distance from where the ceremony had taken place.

I was curious to see who was behind the curtain and listen to more of their fantastic sounds after I'd finished with the ceremony. Now, mind you; I'd performed my ceremony at many weddings and had not yet heard this kind of music before. Simply put, it was the classical kind of music that warms your heart and makes you want to sing and dance. It was the music of my generation.

I left the ceremony location and headed toward the area where the music was coming from. That's when I saw a group of eight musicians, two of which were their main artists - one girl and one guy - singing and playing their instruments while the other six in the band played and sang along with them.

They were fantastic! So much so that I grabbed a glass of fine Merlot wine, pulled up a chair, and listened.

In about 15 minutes, when their set was over, I got up and walked over to Harry, the leader of the group, and complimented him on his fine and entertaining music. I told him I'd performed my ceremony at many weddings and had never heard such great music. In fact, I'd felt like I was sitting in a New York theater listening to the "Jersey Boys," music I remembered so well from my early days.

He smiled, thanked me, and said: "I've played our music at many weddings and have never heard a ceremony like yours, so whenever I plan to get married, you'll be the first on my list of people to call."

I returned the smile and handed him my card just as he handed me his. "I'll see you at your wedding," I said.

Two years later, I received a phone call at my office.

"Hello. This is Captain Arnold. Can I help you?"

"Hi, Captain. This is Harry. How are you?"

The person on the other end of the line sounded like he knew me pretty well, but I was at a loss myself. I paused for a few seconds, trying to remember who "Harry" was.

Before I could ask, I thought he knew that I'd forgotten. "Do you remember 'the Jersey Boys' from the wedding I did at the Lighthouse a few years ago?" he asked.

"Of course, of course! That's all I needed to hear," I replied. "You've said the magic words: 'Jersey Boys'! How've you been? Keeping busy, Harry?"

"I'm always busy, but I'm getting married. I remembered saying I'd call you whenever that happens."

"Yep, I remember. I guess you found the right girl, and it only took you 2 years. Not bad!"

"No, we've known each other longer than that! We just thought it was about time. I told her about you, and she said, 'If he impressed you this much and you feel this strongly about him performing our ceremony, let's get him.'"

I asked Harry about the wedding ceremony's date, time, and location, and he informed me that it was scheduled for 7:30 PM on July 21, 2007, at the Garden City Hotel.

I looked at my calendar with my fingers crossed because this was short notice. Sure enough, I saw that I'd already had a wedding booked at 5:30 in New York City on that day. His would be a tough one to get to, especially with the traffic that's always around when driving out to Long Island on a Saturday night.

"Harry, I'd love to do the ceremony, but I have a bit of a problem," I said. "You see, I'm booked to do a ceremony that same day at 5:30 at the Roosevelt Hotel in the city.

"I know the ceremony will start on time, perhaps even a few minutes early, because the couple has a plane to catch. They're planning to leave for a European honeymoon, and I know they don't want to miss their flight. I figure if I can start my ceremony at 5:30 sharp, I should be able to make it to you in time, but I can't guarantee it because of the traffic I may run into."

"That's fine, Captain," Harry replied. "I will hold up the start of the ceremony until you arrive, no matter what. Just stay in touch along the way, so I know where you are in your travels and when I can expect you to get here."

"Thank God for cell phones," I thought.

Harry also apologized for not contacting me sooner. He admitted that calling just two months before the wedding was a gamble, but he was happy to know that I could be there even if I'd be a little late.

WEDDING CHRONICLES

The date of the wedding came quickly enough, and while waiting at the Roosevelt Hotel for my earlier ceremony that day, I kept looking at my watch.

The wedding for this couple started about 5 minutes earlier than scheduled thanks to the maîtred' and my requests. I emphasized the fact that the couple had to catch a flight, stating how I thought the earlier time would also take some pressure off them. He agreed and moved everything along for an early start, especially since all the guests were already seated and the couple was ready to go. So far, luck has been on my side.

The ceremony ended at just about 5:45, and it only took 20 minutes without having to perform any of my special ceremony enhancements. I said my goodbyes to the couple and promptly left for the nearby garage where I'd parked my car.

A few people were ahead of me, but I told them I had an emergency and asked if they wouldn't mind if the young valet there got my car before theirs.

"No problem, Captain," they said, "we understand!"

With that, I jumped in front of the line, paid the cashier, and handed the kid 5 bucks, telling him I was in a hurry.

I heard the wheels squeal as the car came down the ramp to where I was standing.

"Fast enough?" the kid asked.

I smiled, got into my car, and drove like a race car driver. However, Unless you can fly, you can't just drive over New York traffic, especially through the Queens Midtown tunnel. Traffic was very heavy, and it seemed like everyone was driving to the same place I was.

I called Harry to tell him where I was and explain how I didn't think I'd get there in time.

"Take your time," he said calmly. "Everyone is having a great time. Please don't rush and be careful driving. I need you to get here in one piece."

"Well, that's nice of him," I thought, relieved of some of the pressure I was under.

At 5 minutes to 8, I arrived at the Garden City Hotel with a sigh of relief. The valet took my car, and I was finally on my way to do my thing.

When I walked into the hotel, it looked like the staff was waiting for me. I was immediately escorted to the area where the groom was.

I walked into a very large room stocked with lots of food, fancy hors d'oeuvres, and drinks that were mostly liquor and champagne. There were also so many people (maybe about 50 or

75) that it almost led me to believe this was where the wedding was going to take place.

But I was wrong. This was just one of the rooms at the place, similar to a bridal suite, except it was called the "groom's suite." Harry's friends and bridal party members were simply there enjoying and celebrating some moments before he "bit the bullet."

As soon as Harry saw me enter the room, I could see him breathe a sigh of relief. He immediately handed me the wedding license. "You need this, don't you?" he said. Being in the business he was in, I was sure he knew the routine.

I had him and his witness sign the license, went through some of the procedures with him, and then asked for his bride's whereabouts.

"I think she's one flight up," he said.

"OK. I have to see her, and then we can prepare for the ceremony."

"Whatever you say. You're the boss!"

It didn't take much longer for me to realize that they'd taken 3 floors of this hotel for their wedding, and now I'd need to find someone to lead me to the bride. I was lucky enough to find a hotel staff member stationed right outside the door who quickly brought me to the bridal suite.

I started getting the feeling that everyone was already having such a wonderful time that they didn't even care about the ceremony. When I arrived at the bridal suite, there were as many people there as there'd been at Harry's, with more food, liquor, champagne, and the whole work all around us.

I looked for a bride that I'd never met nor even spoken to before, but out of the corner of this enormous room, I finally found her. For the first time, walking toward me, I could see Tara, a beautiful bride with a smile on her face.

"Here's my Captain!" she called out to me.

"And here's my bride," I replied. "Are you ready to get married?"

"More than you can imagine."

"Let's get the license signed and do it!"

She found her witness to sign the license, and I told her that I was going to the ceremony location to be sure that everything was set up as I needed.

When I walked into the area where the ceremony was going to take place, I couldn't believe my eyes. There was seating for what looked like hundreds and hundreds of guests, all of which were in another waiting area where they'd be kept before being seated for the ceremony.

The maître d' in charge presently came up to me. "Captain," he said, "Whatever you need, just let me know. I'm at your service."

"Can you tell me when this wedding is supposed to start?" I asked.

"It was scheduled to start at 7:30," he explained, "but Mr. Lowery said he needed to change it to an 8:30 ceremony. He said you may be delayed getting here due to another commitment."

I looked at my watch. "We're just about 5 minutes away now from 'showtime,' so I guess that means soon."

"Oh yes. The guests are on their way in right now, and the bridal attendant is with the bride and her bridesmaids. The other bridal attendant is with the groom and his entourage. Everyone else will be in this room in just a few minutes, so we're pretty much on schedule and ready to go."

As I walked into the room, I was struck by how truly majestic it was, and I still couldn't believe how many seats there were. There was no white runner that led up to the altar as you'd normally see at a wedding. Instead, there were sheets of what looked like 8 x10 slabs of flagstone tile along the way. The arch and flowers were really something to see and were unlike anything I'd seen before at any wedding.

To my left, on a kind of small stage, there were also about

10 or more violinists that were going to play their wedding music with a vocalist leading the pack. You'd have to have seen the whole setup to believe in the beauty of it all.

The guests started their way into this spectacular room, family first, so that they could get down to the front rows, and the room filled faster than I expected. Once everyone was seated, we were ready to go.

Bridal attendants had already moved all the bridal party members, including the groom, just outside the door and into position for the ceremony to begin. The bride was kept hidden from everyone. She'd wanted a traditional ceremony and wouldn't see the groom until he saw her walk down the aisle.

I made my usual announcement for everyone to turn off their cell phones. The maître d' looked at me. I gave him a thumbs-up, and the ceremony began.

Beautiful music echoed throughout the room by the strings of the violinists during the processional. The groom came up close to the table between us and waited until all the bridal party had entered.

In a low voice, I asked, "How are you doing?"

"I can't wait," he whispered back.

At that moment, I got the final thumbs up from the maître d' that the bride was ready to enter. At that moment, the violins began to play "Ave Maria," and a vocalist with the voice of an angel began to sing.

"Ladies and Gentlemen, will you please rise for the bride," echoed throughout the room.

Tara came down the aisle by herself and looked like a princess out of a storybook.

I waited until she got to about 25 feet from where Harry was, and then I called out, "Tara, stop right there. Harry, go get your bride!"

The guests' reactions filled the room with oohs and ahhs, and as Harry went to get her, all their hankies and tissues came out, and I hadn't even started my ceremony yet.

After my benediction and blessing at the end of the ceremony, and right after I declared the couple husband and wife, I said, "Harry, you may kiss your bride for as long as you want."

Applause and cheers immediately filled the room.

The ceremony took exactly 29 minutes and 30 seconds. I know because I had a little clock with a timer pasted inside a little black book that I'd left open on the table before us.

There was no receiving line, as you may find at many weddings after a ceremony. This couple left first, right out of the door where they'd made their entrance. From there, they were shuffled off to Tara's bridal suite to be alone with each other for a little while.

I think every married couple needs this to get used to the fact that they're now married and will spend their time together for the rest of their lives. The door to this room is therefore closed to everyone else but me. Ah, the privilege of being a wedding officiant!

When I entered, Tara and Harry hugged and kissed me, thanking me for making this a day they'll always remember. Harry asked me to stay for dinner, but I declined.

"I'd love to," I told them, "but if I were to stay for every wedding dinner that my couples invited me to, I would no longer fit into my uniform, and I just can't have that."

They laughed. "You must stay for the cocktail hour," they said, "you'll love it!"

"Agreed," I said as I left the room to give them some alone time.

"Where is the cocktail hour being held?" I asked one of the hotel staff.

"It's at the rotunda," he said, "but I'll be happy to escort you."

When I arrived, I was greeted by many guests thanking me for the most beautiful ceremony they'd ever seen (I get that a lot, but it's still always good to hear).

WEDDING CHRONICLES

Once I got a chance to look around, I was amazed again to see the setup. This was a very large, round room with 6 other nicely sized rooms extending off from it. Each of these rooms had a different kind of cuisine being served. One room had Italian food, another had Chinese food, yet another had French food, and the others had Spanish food, Greek food, and good old American food. It was really a sight to see!

But perhaps the most amazing thing that sticks out in my mind to this day was this pretty 15-foot lady. She looked like she was standing in the center of this large rotunda room, her hair sitting high up into the chandelier, looking down at all the guests picking away her dress.

After careful examination, I found that she was sitting on a ladder to give the impression that she was standing. Pinned onto her dress, which was about 10 feet long below her waist, were the seating cards for more than 450 guests.

I have a photo (below) of her. As much as I was impressed with her, I think she was just as impressed with me, but it might have been the uniform.

When the cocktail hour was over, trumpets blew, and it was time for each of the guests to make their way into the main dining room.

Since I wouldn't be staying for dinner, I decided to peek at the room and the menu. Filet mignon, lobster tail, Chilean sea bass and dove sole were just a few of the items listed. I should have stayed, but I'll know better next time.

I looked up to see where the music was coming from, and they must have had a 20-piece orchestra. The flowers on the tables were just too beautiful to be real, but they were, and from what I heard from the maître d', there was much more entertainment waiting in the wings.

As I walked out of the hotel and gave my parking ticket to the valet, I asked myself if I'd ever see another wedding like this one. I'm sure I will. I have a lot ahead of me!

When I arrived home, I told my wife all about it. Every detail from beginning to end, so as to create a picture in her mind of exactly what I saw. I even showed her a few of the photos I'd taken with my iPhone to confirm what I'd told her about the "seating card lady".

The next morning, my wife left our apartment to do a little shopping. When she stepped into the elevator, she met Jennifer, one of our neighbors whom I'd never met myself. They were both heading for the garage in our building, where their cars were parked.

My wife asked her if she was going to a party because she was all dressed up.

"No," she said. "I'm not sure if you'd call it a party, but I must go to a wedding breakfast that my nephew is having for the family.

"I was at a wedding last night like you wouldn't believe!" she went on to say. "It was an unforgettable experience. My nephew is in the entertainment business, and I think he had about 500 guests there. The food was so incredible and plentiful, I wished I'd brought a shopping bag."

My wife laughed.

"They had a very tall lady with all these seating cards attached to her dress, and it was a sight to behold! But I think the ceremony was the most important and moving part of that evening.

"They had a Captain perform the ceremony; he was the best I've ever seen. He made us laugh, and he made us smile. He also made us cry. He used words that everyone related to, words that touched your heart. If I ever get married again, I'd call him in a heartbeat."

Just as they got to the garage, my wife smiled, "If you'd like to meet him, just knock on my door. That Captain is my husband."

The Seating Card Lady

WEDDING CHRONICLES

A Surprise Wedding with Some Jail House Blues!

What unfolded from this next story is truly amazing and, without question, deserves a place in my "unique and unusual" weddings. Here is the story of the wonderful wedding one young man orchestrated to pleasantly surprise the love of his life.

The very first time I heard from Jim was by email on November 29, 2007. He explained to me that he wanted to surprise his girlfriend, Jenny, by proposing to her on top of the Empire State Building. He also wanted to marry her while they were there and surprise the wedding.

He was planning to bring Jenny to New York on the pretense of celebrating her 40th birthday. This was to be top secret stuff, and Jim wanted me to communicate with him only at his office or through a special phone number.

Jim and Jenny have had a long and beautiful relationship. Both had been dating steadily for 17 years. To quote his best man: "And we thought lobsters had a long courtship."

Throughout the summer of 2007, Jim was constantly thinking about what he could get Jenny for her upcoming 40th birthday on January 20, 2008. He wanted something that would show her how much she meant to him and how much he loved her. Essentially, he wanted the perfect present for the perfect soul mate.

CAPTAIN ARNOLD WONSEVER

He liked the idea of a surprise wedding in New York City, and since "marriage" wasn't a word that had crossed their lips too much in the past 17 years, he decided to hatch an incredible plan.

In November, Jim started to ask people if they would be interested in joining him and Jenny in New York for their surprise wedding, which he planned to pull off without Jenny knowing. In order to do that, Jim had checked Jenny's cell phone and stole some of the mobile numbers of her closest friends.

Now, remember that Jim and Jenny lived in England, as did their families and friends. He initially thought it would be quite a show if he could get around 20 people to come to the wedding.

Two weeks later, Jim had 42 people on board!

They certainly had family and friends who were happy to participate in this fantastic surprise that Jim had orchestrated for Jenny. Across the oceans, they would come. The wheels began to turn, and everything was set in motion.

Tim's friend, Aly, was vacationing in New York, so she found and booked a hotel for Jim and Jenny on 34th Street. In the meantime, Jim booked the flights and painstakingly browsed the internet for a wedding officiant.

That was when Jim came upon my website. The accolades and praise in the beautiful notes and letters from couples I had married convinced him that I was the man he wanted to perform in his wedding ceremony.

When Jim first contacted me, he said, "I shall be looking for an outdoor wedding at some kind of famous New York landmark, as it's been a city close to both of our hearts. We have been admiring Belvedere Castle in Central Park. Is this a possible venue?"

I told him it was, and so were several other beautiful locations in the Park, but he'd better have a "plan B" in effect. Having a wedding in Central Park at that time of the year could be a problem if the weather wasn't in our favor.

While he struggled to find another venue for the wedding, he was tipped off about The Tavern on the Green in Central Park. After emails too numerous to count, he had the Rafters Room booked, the flowers ordered, and the menu arranged. Another major step had been accomplished in this beautiful plan.

At midnight on New Year's Eve, Jim told Jenny he was taking her to New York for her 40th birthday. She was over the moon, as he put it. He never mentioned anything about marriage or the wedding plans he'd set in motion.

As far as Jenny knew, she was coming to New York just to celebrate her birthday. "What a wonderful birthday present," she thought.

Jim and Jenny landed in New York at mid-day on January 15. He called me then to stay in touch and let me know they were in the neighborhood.

That evening, he took her to the observatory deck on top of the Empire State Building and popped the age-old question.

"Will you marry me?"

She couldn't believe what she was hearing. Three times she asked Jim, "What are you saying that for?"

"Because I want to marry you!" he replied.

Later that evening, Jim told Jenny that if he could arrange everything in time, he may have a venue that would fit them in on Sunday, January 20 (her birthday). He said it would just be a small little wedding, and a pair of strangers for their witnesses suited Jenny just fine.

On Wednesday, January 16, Jim and Jenny took a train to City Hall. They left an hour later with their wedding license in hand.

While at the hotel, Jim secretly browsed the internet for wedding rings and saw a lovely one on the Tiffany & Co website. As the Wall Street store was a stone's throw away from City Hall, they wandered down for a look. Jim found the ring he'd seen for Jenny, and Jenny adored it. She chose a plain band for Jim, which he also loved.

WEDDING CHRONICLES

On Thursday, January 17, they went off in search of wedding outfits. Eight hours of aching legs later, they had chosen their attire.

That Friday, January 18, all 42 of their family and friends had landed in the US by 12 noon. This was the tricky part for Jim - trying to keep in touch with everyone but staying out of their way. Jenny and Jim were only two blocks from the guests' hotel, so they spent the day up by Central Park, keeping as far away as possible from everyone who had come to celebrate this great occasion.

Jim managed to sneak off for half an hour and popped into The Tavern on the Green to finalize some things. He finally got to meet the event's organizer there and dropped off the place cards and seating arrangements. Another important phase was completed with success.

They got back to their hotel at around 4 PM. He now dropped the bombshell on Jenny that he couldn't get the venue he wanted for their wedding, and no matter how hard he tried, he just couldn't find the right place that he felt would be perfect for their wedding day.

On that note, he told Jenny that they would have to return to New York in a month, but this time they'd have some friends to share in their wedding day. Jim could see the disappointment on her face. He told me later that it was cruel but fun!

At 7:30 PM, they headed off to Houston's Bar on Park Avenue for what Jenny thought was to be a few drinks "out and about." By this time, everyone on the trip was waiting across the Street on what was an extremely cold night.

Jim and Jenny went into the bar and found the perfect spot, on a raised section, right in front of the revolving doors and big windows.

Given the freezing weather outside, Jim quickly sent a text message to let everyone know that Jenny's back was to the door and window. "NOW," he texted.

Over her shoulder, Jim could see everyone streaming across the Street. He told me it was amazing, like something from a movie.

Jim then said to Jenny, "I think we should get married on Sunday."

"Oh," came her reply, "OK. But where?"

"Err…I don't know," he said uncertainly. "Let's ask some of these people standing behind you. They're New Yorkers. They know just about everything."

Jim spun her around to come face-to-face with her family, his family, and all their friends. Jenny thought she was dreaming, tried to hide behind Jim, and said she felt as though she was going to be sick with shock. Again, Jim said it was cruel but fun.

It was a truly fantastic, memorable moment, and Jenny later said she loved it. It was then that Jim confessed everything to Jenny and how he'd hatched this plan of his. It brought tears to her eyes.

A short while later, after the surprise and everything had calmed down a little, all the men left for the bachelor party and the ladies for the bachelorette party. Jim had organized the men to go to the Lower East Side and then to Webster Hall.

All went well until they entered Webster Hall. They paid for a reserved table in the VIP area with a complimentary bottle of vodka.

Jim would never be a member of the "Rat Pack Drinking Association," as he called them. Some people have hollow legs when it comes to consuming alcohol, but I could see that Jim was not one of them.

In a slightly inebriated state (mind you, I said slightly), Jim picked up the wrong bottle of vodka and poured himself a drink. He was immediately accosted by its real owners and was told he owed them $225!!

When he refused to pay that, the manager was called but also stated he should pay the $225. He said it was an honest mistake, apologized, and offered to replenish the drink from his own bottle. But his apology was not accepted, and they continued to harass him.

Jim told the manager that he should leave him alone and retreat forthwith (or words to that effect). In a split second, Jim had grown a 6-foot bouncer on each arm. Being the consummate gentlemen they were, they kindly escorted Jim to the exit.

Jim told me that at that moment, he was beginning to think that the club was predominantly attended by amateur wrestlers and football players. As Jim was only 5' 9" and weighed only 168 pounds, he couldn't quite cope with the twisting of his hand and the breaking of his scaphoid bone.

He struggled to break free, and a third bouncer (an amateur boxer?) thought he would try out his right jab twice - first on the back of Jim's head and then in the ribs (possibly a left/right combo?). It looked like this was going to be an HBO fight night, and you didn't even need a ticket!

Someone unbeknownst to Jim then gave this brute a crack to the nose, managing to break it. Mr. "Left Arm Bouncer" and his accomplice, Mr. "Right Arm Bouncer," then thought it would be fun to lay Jim on the curb outside and try some surfboard practice…with him as the surfboard. Fair play to them. Rockaway Beach had only recently been opened, and who was Jim to stand in the way of the next Kelly Slater?

Side note: I later learned that Kelly Slater is a successful professional surfer. Slater is an eight-time world champion and is considered to be somewhat of a legend when it comes to surfing. Just goes to show you how much I know about the subject. I'd rather be running a ship than a surfboard!

Now thinking back, as Jim put it, his head was a little fuzzy, and he might have told them that this was his 4th trip to New York. He had seen all the sights, so they kindly offered him a trip to New York's Finest, and he was welcome to spend the next 24 hours in jail.

Jim's all-inclusive, 24-hour trip came with a free lunch (2 rounds of white bread – no butter, a cheese slice, and a small carton of milk), a free photo (taken from the front and also from the side), a copy of his own fingerprints (should he sometime, in the future, forget who he is), an evening meal (2 rounds of white bread – no butter, another cheese slice, and another small carton of milk) and, last but not least, a room with a view (unfortunately shared with some shady-looking characters).

How could Jim ever forget the fun he had with the NYPD? They were sharing humorous jokes with him and his new-found jailhouse buddies, the best being the one about the Judge not working on a Sunday, and coupled with the Martin Luther King Jr. holiday on Monday, he wouldn't be released until Tuesday. Jim nearly wet himself with laughter (which was a good thing as the toilet had no seat, sick all over it, and 17 attentive fellow inmates). Oh, how they laughed and cried at the same time.

Now Jim had heard of "zero tolerance," and, coming from a

country with a spiraling crime rate, certainly agreed with it. Nothing could have prepared Jim for the "Public Enemy Number 1's" he was about to meet. One chap had committed the heinous crime of drinking a can of beer in the Street. Another had been $6 short on his taxi fare and, despite having left his wallet with the driver, had been arrested when returning with the shortfall. Maybe Jim should have taken these jail tales with a pinch of salt, but the crimes were generally of the same level.

On a more serious note, Jim was charged with the misdemeanor of Assault in the 3rd degree and had to return to New York City to face the Judge on March 27.

On Saturday, January 19, Jim was missing in action until 11:30 PM, when he was finally released. I'm sure you could imagine how Jenny and family were distraught with worry all day and night.

It was soon Sunday, January 20, Jenny's 40th birthday and their wedding day. Jenny later said that the subject of her birthday was the last thing on her mind.

"We were both just thankful that Jim and I were going to make it down the aisle," she said.

The sky was blue, and although it was reportedly -4 degrees, the weather was perfect. After a much-needed night's sleep, Jim and Jenny got themselves ready at their hotel and took a yellow cab to Central Park for midday. They were met by me. Not yet realizing what had happened other than this wedding being a surprise, I eased their nerves immediately and ran through a few procedures.

The rest went "swimmingly well" (to use an English term), considering they had no rehearsals as one would expect under a normal pre-wedding plan. There were quite a few tears shed, mainly by the bride herself, who was somewhat overwhelmed by the whole ceremony.

Fortunately, there was a well-stocked bar waiting to supply everyone with champers (another English term I learned for champagne). The guests enjoyed a beautifully prepared meal in a fantastic setting overlooking the Park and then later carried on the celebrations into the night around some bars in the city – with no drama this time!

The day of the wedding and after the ceremony, I asked Jim how everything went with the surprise he had planned for Jenny. It was then that he took me aside and told me this incredible story and the sequence of events that led up to his arrest.

"You don't know half of it," he said. "I spent almost the last 24 hours in jail and didn't get out until 11:30 last night."

The somewhat happy conclusion following Jim's final meeting with the Judge in March is perfectly described by him in the detailed letter below. What could have been disastrous luckily ended well with some help from a wonderful "Public Defender" and a not-so-grumpy Judge. Jim and Jenny can now return to New York to celebrate their first anniversary and perhaps even renew their vows!

WEDDING CHRONICLES

Dear Captain Arnold,

Thanks for contacting us again. Well, the story did end quite well, if you can call it that.

But the two months at home, while we waited to return for the court hearing, were rather miserable, to say the least, considering it was supposed to be the happiest time of our lives!

Jenny and I were so anxious about the prospect of me returning to the US and being banged up that it left us with a rather dark cloud hanging over us both. I had contacted various US lawyers who quoted extortionate costs for representing me that would've wiped us out. Nevertheless, I was still convinced that returning to face the music was the best option because, as I've said before, we love New York so much I didn't want to run the risk of never being able to return.

Anyway, the day before we left, I found a small bit of info via the internet about my hearing schedule and that I'd been assigned a Public Defender by the name of Christina Darcy. This was the young lady who had interviewed me when I was originally arrested, so I telephoned her to say we were flying over the next day, the day before the hearing on March 27.

We had a brief chat, and she told me to ring her when we arrived. I can't tell you how relieved I was to know that I had someone legal representing me on the other side. The journey went according to plan, and I rang Christina as soon as we touched down in the US.

To my surprise, she told me that she had already liaised with the Judge and had possibly arranged a pre-hearing deal. I was still to attend court as instructed, but the Judge had agreed to reduce the charge of Assault to a charge of Disorderly Conduct, and my sentence was to be.... wait for it.... two days community service!

I nearly collapsed. This, I had not anticipated. She said that it wasn't definite and could quite easily change depending on what side of the bed the Judge got out of, but I didn't care - I was over the moon! I knew we were being a tad premature, but Jenny was so excited we immediately dropped our bags at the hotel and went for some celebratory beer.

The following day was a bizarre experience. I have never been in this sort of situation before in the UK, never mind in a foreign country, and it isn't something that I wish to experience again. The court situation is quite different over here. Here, you appear solely in the courtroom with the Judge or magistrate.

We were amazed to see about 50 or so defendants all in the same room being called up to the front one by one, where you answered your charges. Some guys were escorted in and out in handcuffs, and it was all very solemn. It seemed like an eternity, but I was eventually summoned to the front, where Christina joined me.

WEDDING CHRONICLES

To be honest, it was all over very quickly. I can't remember exactly what was said, but I do remember the Judge smirking as he spoke to me, almost as if to say, "Why the hell have you returned?"

True enough, I was asked if I was prepared to repay the community with two days' work which I could complete over the following days before our flight home on the Sunday. I agreed and left the Courthouse relieved, to say the least. I got my instructions before leaving and then I had to go on a rather unusual shopping spree...to buy work clothes!

As I'd no idea this was going to be the outcome, I'd only taken my suit (for the hearing) and some decent stuff, as you do when you're going on a trip. So I bought some gear, work boots, gloves, a coat, and a hat (it was still cold) and prepared myself for two days of hard graft.

I toddled off at 7 AM the following morning to meet my new workmates in Tompkins Park, East 10th Street. Jenny waved me off and then went back to bed. She had a serious day of shopping ahead of her.

I met the rest of the criminals, and we were duly given the tasks for the day, mainly picking up cigarette butts and litter. I mated up with a guy called Steve, who was from the Bronx. We swapped our criminal stories, and he enlightened me about life in New York City. It wouldn't be ethical to mention what he'd done or some of the others in case their loved ones or employers come across this story.

Anyway, the top and bottom of it is this: I've always wanted to work in New York, and now I have. Even though it's missing the point, I completely enjoyed the two days. Oh! By the way, I spent the second day in the Park picking up dog-pooh. Nice.

It was another one of life's experiences, but I wish our wedding day hadn't been marked as it was. I didn't feel I was completely there in spirit, so maybe one day we'll renew our vows there without getting arrested. It makes for a good story, anyway.

I hope this fills your gap for the end, and next time we're in Manhattan, we shall get in touch, and maybe we can meet up for a beer.

Thanks for ALL you did, Captain Arnold. Take care.

Jim and Jenny

And NO, this story doesn't even end here. I suspected it would continue for many more years, and I was right. They are indeed a very "special" couple.

On October 31, 2017, I received the following email from Jim. I was very surprised by his extremely generous offer. I guess I must've impressed them. Wouldn't you agree?

10/31/2017 **Contact Captain - MAIN**

NAME: Jim

EMAIL: Jim.xxxxx@xxxxxxxl.com

PHONE: (079) xxx-xxxx

MESSAGE:

> *Hi Captain Arnold.*
>
> *You married my wife and me at Tavern on the Green in January 2007. I had an extraordinary story that appeared on your website. My wife and I are from England, and I got arrested at my Bachelor party. That arrest ruined my wedding, and I have never confessed to anyone how I felt.*
>
> *I now wish to renew my vows in Amsterdam. It's a fantastic city, surrounded by water, which reminds me why I require a sea captain. Would you & your*

spouse be willing to fly to Amsterdam, Netherlands, and stay in the Hilton Amsterdam, at my expense, to surprise my wife for the 2nd time for our 10th anniversary?

My contact number is +44 7980 XXXXXX. Just in case there was any confusion, our wedding is on your website:

"A Surprise Wedding with Jail House Blues!"

I replied, calling Jim and telling him that I had to decline his generous offer because my wife was too ill to travel due to a serious medical condition.

I further told him that they could always contact me when they visit New York again. I'd be happy to do a vow renewal as my wedding gift at the top of the Empire State Building, the same spot he proposed to Jenny and where this story all began. By the way, they're thinking about it.

WEDDING CHRONICLES

CAPTAIN ARNOLD WONSEVER

Good Morning America's First Flash Wedding!

It was about 4 PM on Thursday, February 7, 2013, when my cell phone rang. I had just stepped out of my car on my way into the Gramercy Park Hotel to perform a 5 PM wedding ceremony for a couple from Norway.

"Hi, Captain Arnold," a voice on the other end said, "my name is Tyler Brenner and I'm a producer for *Good Morning America*. We wanted to know if you were available to perform a wedding ceremony on our show next week on Valentine's Day.

"I know that it's short notice, but you were highly recommended to us by *New York Magazine,* and this is going to be a surprise wedding for a couple that won a contest held on our show. The bride doesn't know that the groom will be proposing to her in front of millions of viewers, so it should be very interesting and entertaining, to say the least."

I looked at my watch and noticed I still had some time before my next ceremony, so I got back into my car and switched the call to my phone. This was a call that I wanted to concentrate on.

I quickly looked at my schedule and replied, "Sure, I'm available, so long as it's during the morning or daytime. I have to perform a mass vow renewal on the Red Steps in Time Square that evening for hundreds of couples from around the world, and it will be televised as well."

I also explained to Tyler that I was just on my way to perform a ceremony and didn't have too much time to talk but would like to get a few more details. Perhaps we could continue the discussion later or the following day.

"Sure, I understand," she replied, adding, "I can email you some details along with a standard release form that our legal department requires."

"That's fine," I said, "but for now, I just have a few questions so that I can prepare for this wedding. Can you tell me how long the ceremony has to be? Does it have to be approved, and do I have the opportunity to talk to the couple prior to the ceremony?"

Tyler told me that the time of the ceremony had to be limited to five minutes and that their legal department would have to review and approve the ceremony. As far as talking to the couple, that wasn't possible as this was a surprise wedding for the bride.

"The groom will propose to her in the street in front of our studio, and about 30 minutes later, the wedding will take place inside the studio, which has been set up beautifully for a nationally televised wedding. We're all very excited about this event as this has been planned for some time, and everything has been timed perfectly. We have a beautiful wedding cake that has already been designed and a wonderful selection of wedding gowns for the bride to choose from."

"Whew," I thought to myself, "that's a lot to absorb!"

In the few minutes we were talking, I had a lot to think about regarding the preparation required for this, with only a little more than a week away. I thanked Tyler for the update, and we said our goodbyes.

I looked at my watch again and realized that the time just flew by. It was getting close to the scheduled ceremony time for my couple from Norway. I rushed into the Gramercy Park Hotel. I told the desk clerk I was there to perform a wedding and was handed a private elevator key card.

The elevator gave me entrance to a beautiful penthouse suite where I met my lovely couple and their daughter. I still had eight minutes to spare. We spoke for a while, went over the details of the ceremony, and had some of the hotel staff sign the wedding license as witnesses to the wedding.

Moments before the ceremony, the couple and I stood before a large floor-to-ceiling window overlooking the lights of the city. They told me that this was a very big deal for them, having come all the way from Norway with their daughter to be married in the Big Apple, the greatest city in the world!

The ceremony was beautiful, and they loved every moment of it. Little did they know that, just before I entered the hotel, I had received a call from *Good Morning America*. Soon I would perform my ceremony on a national TV show that would be seen by millions of people across the country. To be honest, it kind of blew my mind. After all, it doesn't get much better or bigger than that, does it?

I left the hotel, got back into my car, and kept thinking about the call from Tyler. I didn't have to think long as the phone rang, and I could see on the caller ID that it was Tyler calling me again. I found a spot to pull over at the side of the road so I could again give full focus to the call.

"Captain," she said, "we need you to do a two-minute ceremony. Can you do that?"

I smiled to myself for a moment, thought about it, and then asked her, "How many viewers do you have?"

"About six million, give or take a few," she said.

"Heck, I'll do a 30-second ceremony if you want me to."

Tyler laughed and told me that two minutes of talking is like a lifetime on national TV.

The truth is, she didn't have to tell me that. I already knew it.

I told her that my ceremony usually takes about 18 minutes and 22 seconds. Not too short and not too long, according to my years of experience and what's expected from most wedding venues and catering facilities. I knew that cutting my ceremony down to five minutes would be tough enough, but to further chop it down to only two minutes would be almost impossible if I wanted to keep some of my heartfelt words in.

I told her, however, that nothing was impossible! I'd work on it and email her what I thought would please the producers, the director, and their legal department as well.

"Thank you, Captain," she said graciously, "I know you will. That's why they said you're the best!"

After that, I was left with a lot more to think about on the drive home, not to mention the information that was still missing from this equation.

When I arrived home, I told my wife and children, and everyone was excited for me. When I gave them the details of what was expected, however, they wondered how it would be possible.

"How can you perform a wedding ceremony in only two minutes? That's just about enough time for you to declare them husband and wife and have them kiss!"

"It's going to be a challenge," I said, "but I think I can do it."

The next morning, I woke early after thinking about this project for most of the night. When I perform my ceremony, I don't read it. I just say it. It just comes out of me, and I ad-lib when I feel I have to. I hold a little black book because it looks good for pictures.

Now and then, I'll glance down at the book because it has a little clock stuck to the inside cover that tells me how I'm doing with time.

But now, I had to dissect my ceremony word for word and put together what I would call a "hiccup" of my ceremony to meet the requirements of *Good Morning America.*

I did just that! I put together the distilled essence, the "meat and feeling" of what I believed to be a perfect wedding ceremony for what *GMA* needed and read it using a timer. It was four minutes, twice the time that I needed. I went back to the drawing board with some more cutting and splicing and using the timer. It was three minutes now, but still too long.

Should I speak faster or cut more, and from where? Again and again, I cut a little here and a word there. I read it again with feeling and the time showed two minutes and five seconds. That was it; this would work! I'd lose five seconds when I did the ring ceremony. I read it over and over and it stayed at two minutes and five seconds. I was happy. It was done and I knew it had the words that would make everyone happy.

I called Tyler. I told her I had the ceremony written for her and that she should send it to her legal department for approval. They accepted it. Now all we had to do was wait until Valentine's Day.

In the meantime, I had some more questions for Tyler. What

time did I have to be at the studio? Where could I park my car? Who did I need to see when I arrived at the studio? Could I bring my office assistant with me? What time would I be finished?

I realized that a lot of planning went into this wedding, and while I only had two minutes to play a part in it, my ceremony was still the "glue" that would make it happen when I said, "You may kiss your bride for as long as you want."

Before even asking Tyler, she gave me the answers. "We'll send a limousine to pick you up as well as take you home or any other place you may need to get to. The limo will pick you up at about 5:30 AM and get you to our studio at about 6:15 AM. I'll meet you when you arrive and bring you to the 'Green Room' where you and your assistant can relax and have some refreshments.

"Someone from our team will bring you to the makeup room prior to going on air, and our director will be there to tell you whatever it is you need to know. Our sound team will wire you and run some sound checks and you'll be ready to go. Believe me, everyone knows who you are and they will have you in position when we're ready to begin the ceremony."

Valentine's day finally arrived. My alarm went off at 4:00 AM, and I really didn't get much sleep as I couldn't help but think about the day that lay ahead of me. Kristin, my assistant, came a little early. I could see that she was just as excited and anxious as I was to be at this historical event that would be taking place in just a few hours. Kristin had worked as my Director of Marketing and Social Media, and she was my "right hand" when it came to marketing and public relations.

The limousine arrived right on schedule. The drive to the *GMA* studio was quick since there was very little traffic on the road that hour of the morning. When we arrived, Tyler's aide greeted us just as we got out of the limousine and escorted us to the main studio.

I met Tyler, and we went over the routine again just to be sure I was familiar with what to expect. She brought us into the "Green Room," where we would wait until called by certain members of her staff. It was a comfortable room with some snacks to nibble on.

There was a large TV tuned to the *GMA* station (naturally) so that we could watch the show when it went on the air. From what we could see, there was a large group of teenage dancers that would be dancing in front of the studio when the groom proposed to his girlfriend.

Of course, the bride-to-be had no idea what to expect or, for that matter, what was going on behind the scenes in preparation for this first-ever wedding event on *GMA*.

The minutes clicked away, and soon the show went live. The ceremony was scheduled to start at 8:30 AM, so we had lots of time before I was needed. I was brought into the makeup room by a staff member for some touchups to keep the reflection from the bright lights to a minimum while the cameras rolled.

The next step was to meet the sound engineer. He wired me up with a very small microphone that was completely hidden from view and ran a few sound checks. All was just fine, and he paid me a compliment by telling me I had a nice speaking voice.

After that, I met the DJ. She was actually the music engineer for the show, and today she'd be playing mostly "wedding music". She reviewed with me what and when she'd play to keep me abreast of what to expect before, during, and after the ceremony.

I have to admit, with the exception of the makeup room, all the stuff going on was really no different than what took place when I performed a regular land or major cruise ship wedding. The only difference was that there were a lot of people running around that specialized in their specific field of work. In other words, there were "experts" so that everything they did would be "perfect". I guess that's why it was!

Soon enough, it was showtime! Everything was in place. The groom had proposed to his girlfriend for all of America to see. She accepted, naturally, as we all knew she would. She was then dressed in a beautiful gown, ready to make her entrance while escorted by her father.

WEDDING CHRONICLES

The director quickly said a few words to me, and I took my place on a small platform at the ceremony location. The guests, some of them family members, and the rest of the staff of *GMA* took their seats. The wedding music started playing, the lights came on, and the cameras started rolling! We were on the air, and America was watching!

Two minutes seemed like two hours, but every now and then, when I glanced down at my little black book, I was tempted to go beyond the prepared two-minute script and do my "real" ceremony. I knew, however, that doing this would really screw up their timing, so I held fast to what I agreed to, still feeling like it was like a two-minute warning you'd see at a football game.

As soon as I said, "Brian, you may kiss your bride for as long as you want" there was loud applause from everyone in the studio. The couple was introduced to America by one of the hosts of the show as, Mr. & Mrs. Dundy, the music played, hugs and kisses were exchanged, and the wedding ceremony was history!

The limousine waited for us downstairs, and I was anxious to get home so I could get a few hours of sleep before my next major event in the city.

I'd later be performing a live vow renewal ceremony for hundreds of couples from around the world. I was sure everyone would be there, and every computer in the world would be tuned in to see it. After all, it would be Valentine's Day, and who wouldn't want to renew their vows on the Red Steps for free? But that's a story for another time.

When I got home, I went into my elevator, pressed the button to my floor, and Frank, a friend of mine who lives in my building, approached me.

"Hey," he said, "didn't I see you on *Good Morning America* this morning?"

"Nope," I replied, smiling, "I just went out for a newspaper."

Five minutes later, my phone rang.

"You son of a gun!" Frank exclaimed. "It *was* you! My wife taped it, and we both just saw it again! Wow…you're famous!"

Later that day, I received so many calls from friends and family telling me how much they enjoyed the show. What really impressed me, though, was that I received a call from someone I didn't know - or at least I thought I didn't.

"Hello. This is Captain Arnold," I said. "Can I help you?"

"My name is Zack," the other voice declared.

I thought for a moment and replied, "The only Zack I knew was a guy that I was friendly with in the Navy about 60 years ago."

"Well, that's me," he replied. "Heck, man! I saw you on

Good Morning America and said to my wife that it had to be you!"

It turns out that Zack was living someplace in Arizona. My phone still rings to this day because of that show.

"Honey, I called out to my wife." Please don't give me any more calls. I must get some sleep, or I'll fall asleep while I'm performing my ceremony this evening. I closed the bedroom door, jumped into my bed, and went out like a light. But that evening was the result of another story that I know you'll love. After all, who doesn't love Valentine's Day?

CAPTAIN ARNOLD WONSEVER

Valentine's Day at Times Square, What a Crowd!

It was early in December 2012, just before the Christmas holidays, when I received a call from Larry Hinkler. He identified himself as the vice president of marketing for the New York Alliance, a company that was founded in 1992 to improve and promote Times Square.

He explained that since that time, the company had helped cultivate the creativity, energy, and edge that have made the area, soon called "the crossroads of the world," an icon of entertainment, culture, and urban life for more than a century.

He went on to say that his organization had recently been thinking about creating an extraordinary event that would be made available that upcoming Valentine's Day right in the heart of Times Square.

As Larry described in detail all the things that his company was responsible for, such as organizing the New Year's Eve ball drop and various dance festivals and other major entertaining events in NYC, I couldn't help but wonder why he'd called me.

"You have been referred to us by **New York Magazine**," he said. "We asked them for someone they could recommend helping plan our Valentine's Day event."

"You see, we're thinking of having the first-ever mass vow renewal ceremony for couples looking to be married right on the iconic Red Steps in Times Square, with all the bells and whistles that would go along with it. I wanted to know if you might be interested in performing the ceremony and giving us some advice on its preparation."

I'd felt that this was coming, and I was cool about it - very cool. In my mind, I knew this could be a big thing, not to mention the high exposure it would mean for me in my industry. After all, this was the kind of publicity you couldn't buy, and the credibility I could derive from it was priceless. I couldn't help but see the potential, so of course, I was very excited. But, as I said, I played it cool.

I asked Larry to hold on a second while I checked to make

sure that this slot on my calendar was open without any previous commitments for Valentine's Day (even though I knew it was). I always have my calendar open on one of the monitors at my desk so I can talk about available wedding dates in an instant if any couple calls.

I confirmed I was free and once again didn't want to seem overanxious and jump on what he needed me for. I just listened to everything he had to say on the subject and said very little except that I thought it was a great idea. I also gave kudos to the person who'd come up with it at his company.

"That was me," he replied.

As we discussed it further, I started to think this could be just the beginning of what could really become a tradition in Times Square. I like to think of New York City as a city of love, and it's an essential part of my business. I could see this ceremony in the cards for NYC, not only for Valentine's Day that was coming up but for the following one next year as well as years after that.

I didn't want to get ahead of myself, though, and tried to stick with the present. It's always nice to dream sometimes, but the reality is a lot better when you get right down to it.

I reminded myself that everything that transpired during this phone conversation was in its infancy. We were just exploring and talking about how the event could play out if his company was serious about making it happen.

There was a lot of planning that needed to be done, and not that much time to do it in. I had a lot of questions to ask, and I felt that they also had a lot of questions to ask of me.

After about 20 minutes of conversation, all of which were focused on how I would see the event happening and what I thought needed to make it work, Larry finally confirmed that he liked my suggestions.

"Can you come to our office for a meeting?" he asked. "I'll have all of my team players involved in the project present also."

"Of course," I said.

With only about 2 and a half months to go until February 14, time was of the essence, and the clock was running. Valentine's day would be here and gone before they knew it. If the plan was going to get off the ground on schedule, the dreaming needed to stop, and the enormous amount of work that would be involved had to begin from where I was sitting.

I arrived at their midtown office about five minutes before our scheduled meeting at 11 AM. I'm never, ever late for a meeting and was hoping Larry and his team wouldn't be either.

I was greeted by a receptionist and politely told to take a seat in their guest waiting area.

"Mr. Hinkler will be with you momentarily," the receptionist said. "He's just finishing up a conference call."

I thanked her, and just as I looked down at my watch and saw it was 11 AM, Larry walked toward me with five members of his team following close behind.

We shook hands, and he guided me into a large conference room where I had the opportunity to meet each member of his team. He had some coffee and soft drinks brought in, and I got a feeling this was going to be a long, productive meeting.

A few minutes later, just before I was about to get comfortable, the president of the company walked into the conference room. He introduced himself, greeted me with a smile and a handshake, and paid me a compliment by saying he'd heard nice things about me. I thanked him, and out the door, he went!

"Well, at least I met the boss," I thought to myself. "Seems like a nice guy." Then I took off my jacket so I could blend in with the crowd and feel like I was starting on equal footing.

At that point, Larry's assistant Ray told me that, right from the beginning, they had about ten wedding officiants that they'd selected to interview and meet to discuss this event. This was just a "look-see" meeting to see if I was their man.

My bubble had burst right there and then. Was I the fifth guy they'd met, or maybe the last, or even the first they were working over? Now I felt I knew the real story - that this meeting would only be a way to see if I could answer their many questions and, in that way, contribute to their planning of what could become a historical recurring Valentine's Day event for years to come.

I felt like getting up, thanking them for the coffee and politely saying, "No, thank you!" I refused to be an information bank or a public library they could feed off of. Maybe I was wrong, but it sure felt like I was there just for them to pick my brain, so I held back and just waited and listened.

I'd been in this situation before; in fact, there were many, many times where I'd had to compete with others for the job I do so well. Heck, I do that every time I speak to a bride and groom about performing their wedding ceremony or to the management of a beautiful land venue that would like me to become their preferred wedding officiant.

After all, there are many, many wedding officiants, ministers, reverends, pastors, priests, rabbis, celebrants, and everyone else that can legally perform a wedding ceremony. The competition is enormous.

And to make matters even more difficult, let's not forget the $10 wedding officiant that gets "ordained" online. Every brother, uncle, friend, sister, father, mother, cousin, nephew or best friend (did I leave anyone out?) that wants to perform a wedding ceremony for whoever wants them to counts as competition too. There's an old saying I'm sure you've heard that applies in that case, however: "you get what you pay for."

After a lot of conversation in the room, a lot of what I felt were silly questions were being asked of me, and they discussed why I'd be the one to take over, take charge, and do the thing that I do best. I needed to sell everyone in that room on me and why I was the best choice out of everyone they'd seen or planned to interview.

"How many of you in this room truly enjoyed sitting through a wedding ceremony that you've attended?" I asked. "Be honest about it."

Only one person in the room raised their hand.

"The reason is simple," I said. "All ceremonies seem to say the same thing, and eventually, if you look around, you'll see many guests with their eyes closed. Some might even walk out to grab a smoke or head to the bathroom. I know because I've been there and, being in the business, I've taken notice. Guests can't wait to get to the buffet or the cocktail hour. I see it at almost every wedding I've attended as a guest.

"But that doesn't happen when I perform a ceremony. Instead, guests come up to me and compliment me on how much they enjoyed it and wished it hadn't ended. When I perform my ceremony, they listen to every word I say and become involved. Many have even said they'd felt like they were renewing their vows."

I told them a little story about the time I performed a ceremony for a huge wedding on the Norwegian Breakaway, a very large cruise ship that sails out of the Port of New York. The couple had about 250 guests, and the ceremony had to be held in the ship's theater.

During the ceremony, there was a specific phrase I used: "you're never too old to hold hands." Just at the moment, I said that, I looked down at the front row and saw an elderly couple grab onto each other's hands. That showed me how people listened to what I'd said and reacted accordingly.

"My ceremony is different, and it's powerful, and I don't have to sell you on that. Just read the letters and testimonials on my website. That should tell you enough of what couples think of me after their wedding."

I was on a roll. I could see that I had their undivided attention, and I wasn't about to stop.

I went on to explain how important a wedding ceremony is and how important the renewal of vows is as well.

"With a renewal of vows ceremony, you have to take a

couple back in time to the day they were first married and paint a beautiful picture of that day," I explained. "For this particular event, you'd have to do this and also have them renew their vows while they're standing next to total strangers from around the world who will also be doing the same thing.

"The person performing this ceremony would therefore have to make each couple feel special like they're the only ones being spoken to. Only an extraordinary person – like myself – can do that."

I saw heads nodding in my favor, so I kept going with some strong follow-up.

"When a couple calls me to perform their wedding ceremony, they're primarily shopping for an officiant. I have no idea how they came to me. Is it a referral from someone I've already married? Maybe they were at a wedding where I'd performed a ceremony and asked for my business card. If that's the case, it's pretty much a closed deal, and I just know they'll retain me.

"But when they're just calling because it's a general referral or they found me on Google, that's another situation. Right from the beginning, I go into a programmed mode and tell them everything they want and need to hear about my ceremony."

I told them how I always emphasized to a couple that their ceremony is essentially the "heart & main event" of their wedding day. The vows a couple says to each other, and the words that I say, are what will always be remembered by them, their families, and their guests long after the first dance and the cutting of the cake has faded from memory.

Other than the couple getting married, the officiant is one of the most important people at a wedding. An officiant is the first person that guests will see when they arrive, so it's critical that he has that unique charisma, captivating voice, and exceptional talent needed to connect with guests immediately.

All these qualities help to set the mood and create an unforgettable atmosphere - one filled with love and beauty - that a couple and their guests will cherish for years to come. That's why they need to be entirely sure they only get the "best of the best" - and that is when I come into the picture.

"I have one final thing I'd like to mention before I take any questions," I continued. "My wife and I will be celebrating our 55th wedding anniversary this year, so I think this makes me better qualified than any officiant you'll interview for this ceremony. I can tell a wedding couple with confidence the ingredients that make up the chemistry for a marriage that can last a lifetime!

"I'll be happy to answer any questions relative to anything I've said here today. If you don't have any now, you can always call me. Here's my card!"

Larry asked around the room. "Questions? Anybody?"

"I think he said it all!" Ray answered.

"Gentlemen, ladies, it was a pleasure meeting you today, and I trust that I've shed some light on the importance that your officiant will have on the success of this event. I wish you luck in your search for the right officiant and remind you that since this is the height of the wedding booking season for next year, my phone is always ringing. While I'm available now, I may not be next week. I suggest you give this search your immediate attention."

With that, I thanked everyone for the courtesy extended to me during our meeting and left the room to head for the exit. Larry followed me out, thanked me for the input, and said he would be in touch.

It was just about noon when I stopped at a local coffee shop to grab a bit of lunch and rethink things I'd said during the meeting. I felt I'd said all that needed to be said for them to reach an intelligent decision as to whether I was their guy.

At any rate, I would know soon enough since I'd put the ball in their court at the very end by telling them I was available for only a limited time. It felt good to use a little "reverse pressure."

I drove through the city, as I do most of the time to head home to my office. The traffic was terrible, so I did a lot of thinking again about the project to see if there was anything else I should've said that would've generated a favorable response before I left.

I eventually figured that nature would take its course, and companies like this just had to follow the itinerary they'd put in place. Right now, it was just a waiting game.

"Patience! Patience, Captain Arnold," I thought to myself. But patience is something I have little of.

I arrived home at about 3:30 PM and told my wife all about the meeting. As I walked into my office, I called out to her. "We'll see," I said.

At 4 PM, my office phone rang. I could see "L. Hinkler" on the caller ID.

I picked up the phone and answered it the way I always did. "Hello! This is Captain Arnold. Can I help you?"

"You sure can, Captain Arnold," the voice on the other end said. "You're our guy!"

"How come it took you so long, Larry?" I asked, smiling. "All kidding aside, I appreciate you getting back to me so quickly. I'd thought for sure that you'd have at least wanted to interview those other officiants before making a final decision. I guess I must've said the right things, but I knew you were in my corner since our phone conversation and from the moment that I walked into your office. I thank you for that."

"The fact of the matter is that when you left, it didn't take long for everyone to agree you were *the* officiant we needed to make this a successful event," Larry explained. "Ray thought you had pizzazz and said your speaking voice sounds great. And John, our public relations guy, said your captain's uniform adds a lot of nice colors that put the spotlight on you. That's what we need!

"Look, we'd already interviewed three officiants before I called you, and my entire team agreed. None of them impressed us the way you did. To top it off, just as we were all ready to take a break, our president returned from lunch. When he stepped into the office, he asked if we'd selected the captain. When we said we did, he smiled!"

"I'm flattered by the kind review I got from your team," I said, "and I appreciate you telling me. So where do we go from here? What's our next move? I don't have to tell you that Valentine's Day is just around the corner. I think your team should start to get things moving forward as quickly as possible."

"You're right," he agreed. "John, our public relations man, is going to issue a press release to the media in the next day or two. Our mass vow renewal ceremony will be breaking news this Valentine's Day, and your name will be included as the officiant performing it. I'm sure you may be contacted, so don't be surprised if you get some calls from the media asking you about it."

"No problem," I said. "I'm used to talking to the media."

"Our travel department is also working on setting up a contest for one lucky couple to win an all-expense paid trip to the Bahamas," he added. "I'm not sure what the details of that contest will consist of at this point, but I'll keep you posted. I'll also let you know the number of couples that will be signing up for this event and send you a list every week of how many couples we have so far and where they're coming from.

"In case you didn't know, we plan to hold this event on the Red Steps in Times Square, and that area can hold quite a lot of people. Our marketing department will be working on putting together everything that will be needed to register couples and create a complete information package that will be given to each couple that signs up."

I then explained to Larry that during a vow renewal ceremony, rings are exchanged just like at a real wedding. Considering that there were so many people participating in this event, I suggested that they supply every couple with fake adjustable rings, which were readily available and very inexpensive. They could also inform couples to leave their real rings at home and in a safe place. This way, there'd be no chance of a couple losing their real wedding rings when the ring ceremony was performed. He agreed and thought it was a good idea.

Weeks passed as the wheels were put into motion.

Everything moved along as planned. Each week Larry sent me an updated list of the number of couples that had scheduled to attend. Their PR department did a great job of keeping on top of this, and the turnout was expected to be a large one.

Everyone was pretty excited. Not only would this be a landmark event for them, but if it was successful, it could become a tradition that would take place every year on Valentine's Day – and hopefully, I'd continue to be part of it.

Weeks passed quickly again, and each week Larry sent me the updated count. By January 15, they had logged over 125 couples, and the marketing department was still doing some heavy promotion to make the public aware of this beautiful ceremony.

"Couples that are planning to visit New York from around the world are planning to be at this event, and the list is growing each day," Larry told me.

Meanwhile, I carefully reviewed my ceremony and tweaked it to be a little more appropriate for a vow renewal of this magnitude rather than an actual wedding. I called it my "ceremony of love," and because same sex-marriages had become legal, I included both "husband and wife" and "partners in life" as necessary terms.

For those of you that may not be aware, same-sex marriage became legally recognized in New York on July 24, 2011, under the Marriage Equality Act, which was passed by the New York State

Legislature on June 24, 2011, and signed by Governor Andrew Cuomo on that same day.

Soon enough, it was February 14, 2013, and Valentine's Day had arrived. It was a hectic day for me, but still very special. When I look back, I can't help but think that it was probably the only day that my ceremony would have been seen around the world.

That day, I was up at 4:00 AM. This was because, in addition to the mass vow renewal, the producers of **Good Morning America** had asked me to perform their first-ever two-minute "flash" wedding on their national TV show (but that's another story elsewhere in this book that I hope you'll enjoy).

Much later, after that, I arrived in New York at around 5:30 PM. I parked my car on West 47th Street, very close to Broadway. As I approached the area where the ceremony was about to take place, I could see the crowd beginning to assemble. Many were already standing on the Red Steps to claim their spot for when the ceremony began.

Larry was there with a team of people from his office, preparing the location with a sound system. An open tent was used for the check-in area for couples to sign in and get their rings, which had been placed into little red velvet pouches that said, "Times Square, Valentine's Day."

There were video cameras all over the place and many

photographers, and I noticed a news media truck with the name "Fox TV" on it. They even had a little refreshment stand for the couples and staff that were there.

Larry spotted me walking toward him. He had a broad smile on his face, so I knew he was happy to see me. He immediately introduced me as the ceremony's officiant to so many people that, to be honest, I can't remember a single one of their names.

The ceremony was scheduled to take place at 7:00 PM sharp. They brought a podium up to the location where I'd be standing and did some sound checks with the microphone. The sound engineer asked that I also do a brief sound check to adjust the volume to my voice.

Time flew by fast, but what was interesting to me was that I met several couples whose wedding ceremony I'd performed, and when they found out I was doing the vow renewal ceremony in Times Square, they showed up for it. I still have no idea how they found out!

When 7:00 PM arrived, it was showtime! The Red Steps were packed with couples, so much so that there was not enough room for all of them. So many of them flowed onto the streets to the side of me and behind me. There had to be over 200 couples ready and excited to be part of this incredible evening.

Rachel stood at the podium and introduced me. She added

some impressive lines, telling the crowd that I'd been a Captain for over 35 years and that I'd also been married for over 55 years.

When she said that, I received a nice round of applause from just about everyone that was there, including some of the curious onlookers standing around and walking by. I guess she wanted to emphasize, just as I had, how qualified I was to perform this vow renewal for the people that had come for it.

As soon as she called out my name, I walked toward the podium. She slipped me a sheet of paper, and for a brief moment, I glanced down at it. I got the message she was trying to convey, then looked at the crowd before me, to my sides, and even behind me.

"Good evening, ladies and gentlemen," I said. "Welcome to Times Square, the crossroads of the world! Before I begin my 'ceremony of love,' I'd like to share some facts about this incredible and historical event with you.

"Here this evening, we have couples that come from around the world - couples that come from Argentina, China, the Dominican Republic, the Philippines, Brazil, Poland, Hungary, the UK, Switzerland, Canada, the Netherlands, Ecuador, and even from way down yonder in Australia. We also have a few people that just live up the block from here. So, as you can see, what we have is real diversity.

"Ladies and gentlemen, amid the hustle and bustle of the

most celebrated city in the world, I'd like to perform for you my ceremony of love and take you back in time, back to when you first stood before your minister, your priest, or your rabbi, back to when you held your loved one close to you and declared your love for one another."

In all, my ceremony took about 16 minutes. At the very end, I said, "I now pronounce you husband and wife and partners in life. You may kiss your partner for as long as you want." There was tremendous applause, music started playing, confetti flew everywhere, and balloons were released.

Afterward, I waited close by in a waiting area they'd set up for a receiving line.

Many of the couples came up to take a photo with me and thanked me. Some said beautiful words to me, and many told me they wished I'd been there to perform their wedding. Some that came up from other countries thanked me in their language. It was quite a reception I received, and it's one I won't forget.

As the crowd of couples began to dissipate, the area was soon the way it always was, with just some New Yorkers sitting on the Red Steps and enjoying the sights and sounds of the city.

Larry and his team then came up to me and congratulated me on a great job. "It was a stellar performance, captain, better than we ever could've expected. After what we've seen here tonight, I know we'll be doing this again next year, so please keep the date open for us."

I did, and he called, so I did it again on Valentine's Day the next year. Many said that this time was better than the first. I'm unsure about that, so I'll have to ask my daughter. She was there for both of them.

WEDDING CHRONICLES

The Great Train Wedding

Just when you think you've seen and done it all, there's always one more thing left to surprise you!

It was Tuesday, November 25, 2014, mid-afternoon, when my office phone rang. On the other end, Dextor, the future groom of the story, simply asked, "I know that it's short notice Captain, but are you available to perform your wedding ceremony for us this Friday?"

"Hmm," I thought to myself, "I hope he's not looking for a Black Friday discount!" I told him to hold on while I checked my calendar. "Sure, I'm available," I replied. "Where is the wedding taking place? Can you give me some more details?"

He told me, without hesitation, that he was doing the wedding on the "N" train.

"On the 'N' train!?" I repeated. "Is this for real, or are you kidding me?"

"Yes sir," he replied, "it's for real!"

"Is your bride with you now?"

"Right beside me," he shot back.

"Great. Put the speaker phone on so you both can hear me. I'll tell you some more about me and some important details about my ceremony. If you like what you hear and see on my website, I'll take you to the next step. Does that sound good to you?"

They answered enthusiastically in the affirmative.

"Then," I added, "due to the short time frame we have until your wedding day, we really must move fast. Can you tell me about the logistics for the wedding and how you planned it out? It is, after all, very unusual and sounds like it will be a very special event, to say the least."

Dextor then revealed his plan and was very confident that it would all work out according to the schedule he laid out for me. "I plan to take the train at the King's Highway subway station in Brooklyn. I'll have my mom and dad with me, together with about 20-30 of our friends. We'll decorate the first subway car the best we can with some wedding bells and some fancy paper to dress the train up a little for a wedding."

"Sonia, my bride, will be getting on the train at the 36th Street station and the ceremony will begin as soon as she gets on the train. We won't have too much time from when I get on until she gets on, so I know we'll have to move very fast to prepare the train for the wedding."

"What's really most important," he added, "is that we want the ring ceremony performed just as we are going over the Manhattan Bridge. We'll all exit at the Canal Street station in New

York and from there, we'll all walk to a bar where a friend of ours works and where we'll continue to celebrate our wedding."

"It seems you have this all planned out, but did you get this cleared and approved by the MTA?"

"Yes," he replied.

I then questioned him as to how he planned to deal with the regular train passengers that would be getting on the train or, for that matter, those that were already there. After all, he didn't rent a private train car, so there were bound to be strangers getting on and off the train while the wedding was taking place. His reply was, once again, simple.

"We'll have our people at all the doors to tell passengers that are getting on that a wedding is going to take place. We'll also hand them a rose and ask if they wouldn't mind moving to another car or to the back of the car that we're in. This way, we can at least leave the front of the car fairly empty where the wedding will be."

"Sounds like a plan," I said, adding, "I sure hope it works out!"

I was beginning to think this might be some newsworthy material for some members of the press. I asked Dextor if he wouldn't mind if I contacted some of the news media to tell them about this wedding on the "N" train. He had no problem with it, so

I made a few calls and stirred up some interest from the *New York Daily News* and Channel 7 TV. Both expressed interest and said they would follow up on it.

Preparations began and I emailed Dextor and Sonia my wedding checklist that would give me all the personal information I needed to prepare for their ceremony. Some phone calls were exchanged, logistics and details were reviewed, and all was in place for what later proved to be a fantastic day for everyone involved in the first wedding ever on the "N" Subway Train.

Black Friday arrived and I left my home early in anticipation of heavy traffic conditions. I was right; it seemed that everyone was out of their homes and into their cars doing their Black Friday shopping for those wild discounts.

I arrived about 15 minutes early and parked my car right in front of the King's Highway Station, which looked like a very old building that needed some heavy-duty face-lifting.

We were all to meet at 3:15 PM. We were to board the 3:35 PM train and meet the bride, who would be all set to board at the 36th Street station. We would therefore have about 15-20 minutes before picking up the bride. Everyone who was supposed to be there showed up a few minutes earlier, including the *Daily News* reporter and her photographer.

We were all right on schedule and as we pulled into each

station before arriving at 36th Street, I was amazed to see how cooperative so many passengers were when asked to move to another car or to the back of the car we were in.

Some were shocked when they were about to enter the train and were approached at the door by a total stranger, flowers in hand.

After they were given a quick explanation as to what was happening, some moved back from entering the train, some waited for another train and some came in, took a flower, and moved to the back.

This was some incredible crowd control, especially on a moving subway train where you only have seconds to make a decision before the doors closed.

Everyone was soon busy decorating, hanging wedding bells, wrapping colorful paper around poles, and hanging straps you hold on to when you're standing on a moving train.

While that was happening, Dextor explained to all the passengers that he was getting married and that his bride would be arriving any minute. He also thanked everyone for understanding and offered a flower to those that didn't receive one as a token of his gratitude, a nice gesture that I know everyone appreciated.

I braced myself against the wall at the very front of the train car and waited. This would be the spot where the ceremony would take place. "Whew!" I thought, "What pressure!"

But everything was going just fine, and our timing was perfect. The decorations were done, and it certainly looked like a wedding train. All we needed now was the bride!

The train finally pulled into the 36th Street station and there she was! Sonia and her bridesmaid boarded at the other end of the car and Sonia walked down the aisle toward Dextor, flanked by friends, family, and train passengers. She was a strikingly pretty, blue-eyed blond girl from Ukraine, where all of her family lived.

She reached out for Dextor's hand to steady herself and they both stood before me, bracing themselves and holding on to a pole that stood between them.

Without missing a beat, the ceremony began. I became acutely aware that time was of the essence. I had to move along as fast as possible, but I still wanted my words to be felt and not have this turn into a circus instead of a heartfelt wedding ceremony.

Even though the noise of the train tracks were beneath our feet and the distraction of a moving train was all around us, when I had Dextor and Sonia repeat their vows to each other, it was then that I saw tears stream from their eyes and knew that my ceremony had hit home. I looked around and saw many of their friends and family wiping their eyes at a moment that was very emotional.

WEDDING CHRONICLES

The best man signaled to me that we were approaching the Manhattan Bridge and it was time for the ring ceremony. Rings were exchanged at the exact location they wanted, and more tears were shed. Just as the train started pulling into the Canal Street station, it was time to declare them husband and wife. "Dextor," I then said, "you may kiss your bride for as long as you want!"

The happy couple kissed to thunderous applause from everyone on the train, so loud that you couldn't even hear the tracks and the screeching sounds of the train. The only other thing you heard was the sound of the conductor's voice coming from the speakers, saying, "Canal Street". It was a magical moment, and you could feel the love and excitement that filled that train car.

Now it was time for us all to get off the train as it was the last stop for the wedding party. Some photos were taken at the Canal Street station and a quick walk took us to their friend's bar, "Winnie's", where the remainder of the celebration most likely continued into the wee hours of the morning.

CAPTAIN ARNOLD WONSEVER

I'm in the New York Times Check the Video!

It was the second week in February 2014 when I received a call from Alice Allen, a feature reporter for the *New York Times*.

"I'm working on a story about captains performing wedding ceremonies on ships", she said. "I was told by someone at *New York Magazine* that you may be able to help me with some of the facts about that for some research I've been doing."

"Wow," I thought to myself. "The **New York Times** is calling me to help with a story. It doesn't get much better than that!"

"Sure", I replied. "Having over 10 years of experience as an exclusive wedding officiant for some of the major cruise ships in the New York area, I think I'm in a pretty good position to help you with your story. I can certainly lead you to some people or places that can assist you as well."

Alice asked many questions at the beginning of our conversation and each question led to some lengthy dialogue between us. It was clear to me that this was going to be a story that would have a lot of detail and would be very interesting and informative for her readers.

When I felt that I couldn't help with a particular question, I referred her to a source that I knew would be better able to supply accurate facts related to her question. I learned a long time ago (after several interviews with the press and other media) that reporters rely on getting truthful and accurate facts when writing or reporting a story, no matter what the media may be.

A few weeks passed and during that time, Alice called every now and then to ask for some additional information. Eventually, I felt that she was nearing the end of her story and would soon have it published, most probably in the wedding section of the *New York Times*.

We developed a nice working relationship while she was writing her story and once we said our goodbyes, she asked if it was possible for her to send a photographer to take a few photos of me for the story. It's not every day that one gets their photo in the *New York Times*!

Then it hit me. I had a great idea that I thought would really work with her story. I told Alice I was scheduled to perform a wedding ceremony on the Skyline Princess, a beautiful luxury motor yacht that sails out of the World's Fair Marina in Flushing, New York. I suggested that her photographer also take a few photos of the wedding ceremony as well as the ship and remain on board to enjoy the cruise when he was finished.

"That would be wonderful," she said. "A few ceremony photos would be a nice finishing touch to the story".

She then put the wheels in motion and worked it right into the short time frame we had. "I have a deadline to meet" seemed to be the famous last line of conversation from most of the reporters that had interviewed me in the past, but not Alice. She was cool and never once mentioned the word "deadline".

Alice also asked me if it was possible for her to call the couple that were getting married so that she could have a brief interview with them and possibly use it in her story. I agreed, but I first wanted to contact the couple for their permission. I emphasized that I did make it a policy to respect the privacy of the couples that retained me to perform their wedding ceremony. Alice understood and appreciated this.

I told her I would get back to her as soon as possible after I reached out to the couple, explained the situation, and cleared it with them.

Within a few hours, I was able to reach the bride. I explained the circumstances and asked if it was okay for Alice to call her and for the photographer to take a few photos of the ceremony.

The bride was ecstatic, excited, and very happy to be part of the story. I called Alice and gave her the "green light" and the contact information so that she could reach the bride.

Not to jump ahead, but the beginning of the interview that

she had with the bride read like this in the *New York Times*:

"Holly Brolsma and Alex Colon, both 28, were married Feb. 15 aboard the Skyline Princess in a ceremony led by Capt. Arnold of Bayside, Queens. ("I always wear my captain's uniform," said the Captain, who has become an ordained minister through a church in Maryland and who notes that he has performed nearly 2,000 marriages since 2003. "The gold stripes impress people.")

The ship (no relation to Princess Cruises) was docked at the World's Fair Marina in Flushing, Queens. After the ceremony, the couple and their 11 guests took a dinner cruise around the city.

"I thought it was appropriate since Captain Arnold was licensed by the Coast Guard and we were in the military," Ms. Brolsma said. "Also, we didn't want to risk it with all the horror stories going on with cruise ships."

Ms. Brolsma, a former Marine, and Mr. Colon, who was in the Air Force, said that because of their military service, they understood the captain was not allowed to marry them at sea unless he had other credentials.

The photographer called me the day before the wedding just to check in with me, confirm the time of the wedding, and get directions to the ship as he was planning to rent a car that didn't have GPS. This made me feel good as it further confirmed that the "photo shoot" was for real.

WEDDING CHRONICLES

The weather report for the day of the wedding, however, was not good at all and held true according to the predictions of all local TV weather channels. When I woke that morning and looked out my window, I could see that it was cold and very windy. Trees were bending in the wind and there was heavy snowfall.

It looked like a blizzard and when I stepped outside, it felt like a blizzard. It was certainly not a day that a bride and groom would welcome as their wedding day, especially when that wedding would be taking place on a motor yacht.

It was important to keep in mind that while this yacht had three spacious, fully heated, and climate-controlled decks, weather conditions always played a big part in how the passengers felt and reacted. It would still be unpleasant to board during nasty weather, which also applied to the big, major cruise ships I'd been on.

Taking all this into consideration, I arrived at the Skyline Princess much earlier than usual. I wanted to see that everything was in order and advise the staff about the *New York Times* photographer coming down to take some photos.

Everyone was happy to hear the news. The couple and their guests arrived right on time; in fact, they'd come a little earlier, even with the inclement weather outside. Everyone seemed very excited about the event and some even said that they wished they'd brought their sleds and skies. They claimed it would have added to the fun of trudging through the snow that kept piling up on the dock!

It was great to see such an upbeat attitude on such a dismal-looking day. Nevertheless, the Skyline Princess sailed rain or shine, and now we could also add snow.

I spent some time with the couple going over the wedding license and had their witnesses sign it. I also quickly reviewed what they could expect during the ceremony and coordinated the wedding music selection with the DJ. It was a mini rehearsal, in a way, and that made them feel very comfortable.

Some comments were made about when the photographer would come to take photos and while on that subject, the bride told me that she had had a wonderful conversation with Alice. She felt that her interview would read very well in Alice's story, and, in the end, it certainly did!

But as time went by, I was getting more and more concerned about the photographer arriving in this bad weather. Maybe he couldn't find us. Maybe the car got stuck in the snow, and maybe he felt it wasn't safe to drive.

Lots of "maybes" crossed my mind, so I went into the wheelhouse. From there, I could look out the window and get a nice, clear view of the long, snow-covered dock before us. I had hoped to see the photographer, but it was to no avail.

I looked at my watch and noticed that there were only about 45 minutes left before the ceremony time. I resolved in my mind that the photographer was going to be a no-show and could only blame the weather for it.

As I started to leave the wheelhouse, however, I noticed a pair of binoculars hanging on the bulkhead and decided to give one last look out the window.

Visibility was very poor with the snow coming down, but as I began to focus the binoculars, I was able to make out an image at the far end of the dock walking toward us. I kept my fingers crossed and hoped it was our guy.

As he got closer, I began to see clearly that he was carrying a bag. He was all bundled up, wearing a hoodie of some sort to protect himself from the driving snow. He was close enough now that I was able to see his face, which was also covered in that same snow.

It had to be Pete, our photographer. Everyone else who was supposed to board had already been accounted for.

I immediately made my way down to the second level and ran ahead to the outside deck, where I was able to shout, "Pete, is that you?"

"Yes, it's me, Captain Arnold," he said, "I finally made it."

I shouted back down to tell him to walk down the gangplank. I'd meet him as he entered the ship.

When Pete walked onto the ship, he looked like a snowman.

"I can't believe you made it," I said. "I thought for sure I would be getting a call from you that the snow bogged you down from getting here."

"We photographers are like the mailman," he replied. "We get through and show up wherever we have to be when we get an assignment, no matter what the weather conditions are."

I believed him - what we had was nothing short of a blizzard! I got him a hot drink, and he got himself warmed up a bit as he began to unpack and put his equipment together.

I told Pete that the ceremony was due to start shortly, but we had just enough time that he didn't need to rush. I also asked how he would like to take his photos and if there was anything he needed from me or a member of the crew. I was not only surprised but elated by his response.

"Captain," he said, "Alice, the reporter that's doing this story, and everyone connected with it (including her editor and our photo editor), thought that it deserved more than just a few photos. They also asked me to shoot some video segments of the wedding ceremony. Even more importantly, they wanted me to shoot a video interview about the weddings you've performed as Captain and anything else you feel would be of interest to our viewers. This video interview will also appear on the *New York Times*' digital website.

"Just so you know," he went on to say, "I believe that their digital website has a larger circulation than their print media does, and it lasts forever. They'll use a photo with the print media, but with digital media, or the 'way of the future,' readers, as well as nonreaders, will be able to see and hear you tell your story.

This may also wake up a lot of people who'll begin to investigate the beauty and benefit of having a wedding or other event on a motor yacht or ship. Oh, you'll be happy, I'm sure of it."

"I wasn't expecting this, Pete," I said excitedly, "and I certainly wasn't prepared for it, but I'll take it anytime." I smiled as I said that and, at the same time, knew that I would just have to "wing it" as far as the interview.

With that reply from me, Pete got his camera set up in hand and said, "I know it's snowing, but I would like to take a few photos of you while you're outside on the front deck as that will also show the ship's name. We'll have to do it now before it gets too dark outside."

"Let's go", I said.

Photos were snapped, and some short videos were taken that pleased him, and then we went back into the wheelhouse where the interview would take place.

The crew and deckhands were alerted that we were not to be disturbed under any condition unless we had to "abandon ship" (a joke, of course). The couple, meanwhile, was made comfortable in the bridal suite and we still had about 25 minutes before the ceremony.

As we got ready to start the interview, Pete, from the outset, knew just what to do and say.

"Captain," he said, "I want you to relax and just be yourself. I know you weren't prepared for this, but you've got a great speaking voice, so just tell your story and I know people will listen."

I did just that and I felt the interview went very well. Pete also said that he captured everything he needed and felt that the reporter, the photo editor, and all the people involved with the story would be very pleased.

The wedding ceremony began, and Pete snapped quite a few photos. He also shot some video that was spliced into the interview.

For the entire time, he stayed at a distance, unlike other photographers that usually climb up right next to you during a ceremony. To be honest, I didn't even know he was there taking photos, and that's the sign of a great photographer.

Soon, the photo and video sessions were over. I asked Pete the question I'm sure most people asked after being interviewed, wondering if he had some idea when this would go live or when the story would appear.

His answer was a simple "no."

"It's up to the powers that be to make those decisions," he said. "It'll only take me several days to work on this with my editor and when I'm finished with the editing, I'll send the finished copy to Alice to look at with her editor. They'll make the final decision when it goes live on the digital website and in the print media."

As he spoke, the ship started up its engines. The Captain for that evening was ready to blast the horns indicating that the ship was leaving the dock and setting sail toward the Statue of Liberty.

I asked Pete if he would like to stay on board, relax, and enjoy the cruise, but due to the bad weather, he thought it would be best if he left to go home before it got worse.

I extended him an invitation to be my guest with his

girlfriend on another dinner cruise when we had warmer weather during the summer months. He agreed and then left the ship.

The Captain blasted the three-horn signal and away we sailed toward the Statue of Liberty. It was a beautiful evening enjoyed by all, but especially by my couple.

After a few weeks had passed, I received an email from Alice.

"I made you a star," she said in her email to me. "We have the video showing now on our digital website, and the story will appear in this Sunday's paper in the 'wedding section.' Go online and check out 'Can a Captain Marry Us?' and you'll see the video. It's terrific."

So, for those of you that don't read *The New York Times*, especially those of you that didn't know they had a digital news website, do yourself a favor and go to your computer or smartphone. Type into your device **"Can a Captain Marry Us?"** and enjoy a two-minute and thirty-one-second video that this Captain will remember for a long, long time.

A version of her article appears in print on March 2, 2014, on page ST17 of the New York edition with the headline: *A Marriage at Sea? Get Me Rewrite*.

Hollywood gave a big boost to the myth that captains could legally join couples on the open seas. In New York, Captain Arnold, an ordained Chaplin, is making this myth a reality. **New York Times *** February 28, 2014**

Just type into your web browser: **A Marriage at Sea? Get Me Rewrite**.

CAPTAIN ARNOLD WONSEVER

The Wedding without a Bride & Groom (almost...)

It was an unusually hot day on May 22, 2009, at almost 90 degrees - the perfect weather for getting married on a sunset dinner cruise aboard the Skyline Princess, a beautiful tri-level motor yacht that was docked at the World's Fair Marina by Citi Field. The bride, Myra, planned to arrive early to supervise the set-up of her perfect day, so my wedding coordinator and I arrived at the World's Fair Marina promptly at 5 pm to meet her and her bridesmaids. As the reception site was set up and we went over details with the crew, I anxiously looked from my watch to the parking area for the bride-to-be's arrival. As the clock ticked away, we still had no bride or groom at 6 pm.

Guests were told to arrive at the pier by 6:30 pm since the ceremony would take place at 7:30 pm on the yacht and then we would set sail at 8 pm. When 6:30 pm was upon us and guests were waiting on the pier, we still had no bride or groom. I was finally able to get hold of the bride on a cell phone to find out she was "just leaving" Newark, NJ. Right then, the panic set in and we knew the odds were stacked against her. She had to make it to the pier where the Skyline Princess was docked in Flushing (Queens), NY, during rush hour traffic on the Friday of Memorial Day Weekend when the Yankees were playing at home in less than an hour – an impossible task for even the most determined driver.

WEDDING CHRONICLES

We braced ourselves for the impending chaos and, at 7 pm, began to board the wedding guests hoping the couple would arrive soon. We watched the minutes tick away. Tick tock, tick tock… 7:15pm… 7:30pm… 7:45pm… Still no bride or groom! We finally received word that the bride was close, so my coordinator waited at the entrance to the pier. At 8 pm, the car arrived with a tearful bride and her bridal party. She explained that she had forgotten her wedding dress and the bridal party dresses were in another car and that the dresses were now with the groom, who was still on his way. The bride was calmed down and quickly rushed to the "bridal suite" on the yacht so she could get her hair and makeup ready while she waited for her dress.

At 8:15 pm, the yacht captain was anxious to set sail just as Alan, the groom, finally arrived. With barely a hello, my coordinator swooped in to take the dresses from the groom and sprinted back across the pier and onto the yacht to get them to the bride and her bridesmaids. and the moment the groom stepped onboard, the yacht set sail into the sunset.

By 8:30 pm, the ceremony began in the romantic light of dusk. The evening breeze blew the worries and chaos of "the wedding that almost wasn't" away. The vows were shared, the couple kissed and the journey of their lives coming together as one began. An evening of dining, dancing, and drinking followed, backlit with dramatic views of the New York City skyline and Lady

CAPTAIN ARNOLD WONSEVER

Liberty's watchful eye. It was an evening no one would ever forget, especially Myra & Alan.

Dear Captain Arnold,

It has taken us a while to write this letter, but we could not go on without expressing our immense gratitude to you and the Skyline Princess crew.

Everything that was said in our agreement was completed flawlessly throughout the wedding. Our guests, family members and we enjoyed the most lovely and exclusive ceremony ever. The cake was marvelous and delicious. The crew always had a pleasant manner. My bouquet was gorgeous, and every single detail of the wedding was better than we'd dreamed of.

All the nervous tension I was feeling went away when I got to the ship and realized you had everything under control.

We would also like to express our appreciation to Alberta, your wedding coordinator. I was almost in tears when I got to the boat 2 hours late and without my wedding gown. Alberta took the time to calm me down with her comforting words and scotch on the rocks! She is the greatest personal wedding coordinator in the world! Everything I'd ever dreamed of about how my wedding would be was possible thanks to you. We are proud to say our wedding was

WEDDING CHRONICLES

absolutely perfect. And I can assure you that everyone that shared this special day with us feels the same way.

Lastly, we wanted to let you know that you were and will always be a very important person in our lives. Your name is even on our wedding certificate! I hope one day we will see each other again, perhaps for our first Anniversary. Who knows?

With sincere love,

Myra & Alan

PS: We loved the package you sent us. It was the very first wedding picture we received.

THE END

CAPTAIN ARNOLD WONSEVER

Questions and Answers

To Help Couples Planning to Get Married

Q) How soon should couples book their date with a wedding Officiant?

A) Immediately following the selection of their wedding location. The couple should understand that the wedding ceremony is truly the most important part of their wedding day. It's the "heart & main event" of that day and it kicks off the reception and everything else that follows. The vows they say to each other, the words the Officiant will say are what will always be remembered by them, family, and guests long after their first dance, the cutting of their wedding cake, or the throwing of the bride's bouquet has faded from memory. So, whoever they get to perform their ceremony, they can be sure they will get the "best of the best" if they begin their search early for a wedding Officiant.

Q) What are customary policies regarding deposits?

A) That depends on the wedding Officiant. Some ask for 50% of their fee, some less and some more. I don't get rich on deposits, so I ask a minimum of $100, and the balance is paid the day of the wedding.

WEDDING CHRONICLES

Q) Is it typical for couples to meet with the wedding Officiant prior to the wedding?

A) With today's conveniences of email, cellphones, and the Internet, I find that most couples don't ask to meet with me because when they contact me, I fully explain the details and highlights of my ceremony, more details about me and what my fee is. I answer all their questions and concerns and I'm always available to my couples 24/7 should they have any additional questions or concerns at a later time. If they like what they hear and what they see on my website, I take them to the next step. I do meet with couples if they request a meeting and a time and place that's usually convenient for the couple and I is arranged.

Q) If a bride and groom are of different faiths, or one of them is not religious, is that a problem?

A) Not at all. I do perform inter-racial, inter-faith ceremonies and of course join many different cultures together as well. My ceremony is <u>non-denominational</u> and deals mostly with what love and marriage are all about. I don't use negative words like, "in sickness or in health" or "till death do you part", after all, the couple is not signing a Mafia contract. It's a happy time so I inject just a bit of humor into my ceremony as I would rather see their guests smile than feel like they were at a funeral.

Q) If the bride and/or the groom was married before, but is now legally divorced, will a wedding Officiant marry them?

A) Yes, I believe an Officiant will perform the wedding ceremony in most cases. But it's highly unlikely that a Priest will perform a ceremony in his church for the couple. But the laws of the church may have changed.

Q) Can children be incorporated into the vows?

A) Most definitely. I encourage it and when I'm talking to the couple I ask if they have children from a previous marriage or an existing relationship and highly recommend that they incorporate children into a ceremony and presenting them with a token of love while some beautiful words are spoken during that part of the ceremony. I have that beautifully described on my website under the link "Wedding Memories": Here is a brief description of the child's ceremony: For a very moving and beautifully performed ceremony that tells a child, or children, how much you love them and how important they are to you, then this is a "must have." This ceremony is for the bride and groom that may already have a young child or children from a former marriage or of their own. On this special wedding day of yours, you are also pledging your love to them as well, committing to them, and promising that you will create a family together. You are letting them know that they are a very important and meaningful part of this union. This will be their "special day" too.

This ceremony is usually performed after the ring ceremony. The words spoken by the Captain express your never-ending love and devotion to the child/children and further reinforce your commitment that you both will always be there for them even as they grow to be young adults. The Captain asks that you both repeat a beautiful vow to your child/children and to conclude the ceremony, a small token of your love, such as a ring, bracelet, or necklace, is presented to the child.

Q) Does the wedding Officiant normally go to the rehearsal?

A) Some do, some don't. I find that an Officiant of any kind, be it a Reverend, Pastor, Minister really can't play a part in the rehearsal as they are usually standing with the groom and the best man at the location of the ceremony waiting for the processional to begin. It's the event planner, Maitre'D or the wedding facility staff that organizes and sends down the processional not the Officiant. Rehearsals are usually done prior to the guests arriving on the same day as the wedding and in my experience not necessary to have a separate day or evening set aside for a rehearsal. It will just cost the couple additional monies. If on the other hand the couple wants a rehearsal coupled together for the sake of having a family get together dinner before the wedding day, that's a different story. Many couples will do that.

Q) How long does the wedding Officiant normally stay after the ceremony?

A) I would like to stay about 15-30 minutes. I chat with the guests a bit and being a Captain, I get a bit of attention that also leads me to answer many questions about cruise ship weddings that guests ask about. I don't like to hit and run when I perform my ceremony, but my time is important since I do perform as many as 3, 4, or more weddings in one day so I have to space them apart to allow my travel time. There are so many times that I'm also invited to the reception dinner with my wife but unfortunately time does not permit, and the couple understands that I may have other obligations.

Q) Does the wedding Officiant wear a traditional robe, or do they dress in other attire?

A) Yes, most Officiants will wear their traditional robe but, in many cases, I've seen them perform a ceremony in a business suit. I have Ministers that work for me on the cruise ships, and they elect to wear a robe. Speaking for myself, I wear my Captain's uniform since I'm a Chaplain and because most of the wedding ceremonies that I perform are in a nautical atmosphere. Most that is, but not all. Seems when a couple is getting married on a ship, at the beach, by a lake, a facility by the water, even a big puddle, they want a Captain to fit into that nautical surrounding. Lucky me!

WEDDING CHRONICLES

Q) How many couples can a wedding Officiant marry at one time?

A) As many as he can I suppose. I've married 3 couples at the same time aboard a ship but there is no restriction to my knowledge so long as the couples have their marriage license. I've been approached to perform a mass vow renewal ceremony in Manhattan, and it was a wonderful event. This was an historical event and the start of mass wedding ceremonies especially on Valentine's Day.

Q) How much are couples typically allowed to customize the ceremony?

A) As much as they want. It's their wedding ceremony and they are paying for it. But in my experience a smart couple leaves it up to the Officiant if they have confidence in him/her and feel comfortable from the onset that they selected the right person to perform their ceremony. It all begins when they first talk to their Officiant and feel secure in the knowledge that they have the right person to perform what will be the most important part of their wedding day. Their ceremony.

Q) Do wedding Officiants allow couples to write their own vows?

A) Ha, or should I say LOL. Couples don't really write vows to one another; they write their feelings. "Oh John, I fell in love with you the first time we met on the roller coaster in Coney Island and I could feel the love you had for me" that kind of stuff. And that's fine.

They will pull out that little piece of paper and read their feelings for one another and when they are finished, I complement that by having them face each other, hold hands, look into each other's eyes, and repeat those words that will bind them together for the rest of their lives. I ask them to repeat 2 to 3 words at a time after me and what I tell them to say in one paragraph says it all. They don't have to worry about studying vows or memorizing anything. I like to keep it stress free and have them enjoy their ceremony.

Q) Will wedding Officiants generally marry couples that are not members of a religious congregation?

A) Of course. I don't see any boundaries with respect to religious beliefs except maybe where the Church may stand on this. There are many couples that don't want me to use the word G-d in my ceremony and I respect their beliefs. I simply use a different blessing at the end of my ceremony. In my opinion, a wedding Officiant will perform a wedding ceremony for any couple no matter what their religious beliefs may be or if they belong to a religious congregation or not.

Q) Are friends allowed to participate in the ceremony, including giving readings, singing, or anything else? How should these things be coordinated with the wedding Officiant?

A) In my ceremony of course they are. I cover this in detail when I first speak with the couple. I also send them a checklist shortly after they retain me for their review. I also send them a final copy of this check list a few weeks prior to their wedding day. This checklist gives me all the information I need to know to personalize their ceremony. Names of loved ones that they may want me to mention in a tribute that I like to do at the beginning of my ceremony, do they want a child's ceremony, if so, I need the names of the child or children, will a friend or relative like to do a reading or will someone be singing, I need their names. This information and more is given to me prior to the wedding day and I incorporate this info into my ceremony so I know when to introduce those individuals that will partake in the ceremony. I speak to my couple prior to the ceremony to review the checklist and cover everything they may be concerned with. There are other wedding enhancements that are also applicable, and I cover it all.

Q) How much do wedding Officiants usually charge for services?

A) That really depends on one key factor. Location of the wedding. Where will the wedding be held and how far does the Officiant have to travel. At City Hall, you could pay $25 for a simple 5-minute ceremony. I believe fees can range from $350 to $1000 further depending on the distance that the Officiant must travel. Some weddings may require long distance travel even on an airline and that would increase their fee substantially...

WEDDING CHRONICLES

About The Author

Meet Captain Arnold Wonsever, a maritime legend with an impressive 48-year career navigating passenger-carrying vessels, backed by an official United States Coast Guard license. Yet, Captain Arnold isn't your typical sea captain; he's a certified ordained chaplain registered with the City Clerk's Office of the City of New York.

Captain Arnold's journey is nothing short of extraordinary, marrying his seafaring expertise with a talent for creating unforgettable wedding ceremonies. His unique touch has graced ceremonies on land, at sea, and even in the sky, leaving couples with indelible memories.

Some unforgettable moments include mass Vow Renewal ceremonies on Times Square's iconic Red Steps, broadcasted globally by the Times Square Alliance. Captain Arnold made history on ABC's Good Morning America with a two-minute flash wedding ceremony watched by a staggering 6 million viewers.

The New York Times recognized Captain Arnold's role in turning the dream of captains legally uniting couples on open seas into a reality. An interview on The New York Times' digital platform offers deeper insights into his incredible journey.

Captain Arnold's expertise transcends officiating; he's earned "Best of Weddings" accolades from couples on The Knot,

Wedding Wire, and LI Wedding Brides. His true gift lies in helping couples personalize their vows, ensuring their special day resonates with genuine emotions.

He specializes in non-denominational, interfaith, interracial, and LGBTQ weddings, spreading joy through second marriages and heartfelt anniversary celebrations with re-affirming vows.

Though he retired as an exclusive wedding officiant for major cruise ships in the New York tri-state area, Captain Arnold's legacy endures in the hearts of families and guests touched by his enchanting ceremonies.

His book, a treasury of love and commitment stories, promises to captivate readers just as writing it delighted Captain Arnold. But the story doesn't end there – Captain Arnold still dons his captain's hat to perform weddings in vibrant New York, Connecticut, and New Jersey areas. You may be fortunate enough to witness his magic at a wedding ceremony one day – and perhaps, it could even be yours! Captain Arnold Wonsever, the captain of love, is committed to making dreams come true, one ceremony at a time.